Praise for *Splinter & Shard*

"The women in these pages walk away from convention, while the men struggle to make sense of the world. I love the ways that shafts of humour and farce pierce the confusion of self-discovery, while Keating's careful attention to landscape and language creates a complete world within each story. A wonderful collection."

— CHARLOTTE GRAY, CM, author of *Passionate Mothers, Powerful Sons: The Lives of Jennie Jerome Churchill and Sara Delano Roosevelt*

"Highest praise for *Splinter & Shard*: hard-boiled and humming with energy. Like the best dance partner, Lulu Keating takes you by the hand, spins you around, keeps you on your toes, and leaves you smitten. More please!"

— LAWRENCE HILL, author of *The Book of Negroes*

"Vivid and evocative, these richly rewarding stories dig deeply into the human experiences of love, loss, and hope."

— ANNA PORTER

"Keating's characters walk in and out of these recorded moments. Authentic and flawed, they are whole people whose lives continue past these infectious stories of resilience, family, lovers, and rough terrain."

— CHARLIE PETCH, author of *Why I Was Late*

Lulu Keating

Splinter & Shard

stories

Dedicated to
Calhoun Keating Malay and Rod Malay
for teaching me about love.

Published by ECW Press
665 Gerrard Street East
Toronto, Ontario, Canada M4M 1Y2
416-694-3348 / info@ecwpress.com

Editor for the Press: Susan Renouf
Copy editor: Crissy Boylan
Cover design: Jo Walker

LIBRARY AND ARCHIVES CANADA CATALOGUING IN PUBLICATION

Title: Splinter & shard : stories / Lulu Keating.

Other titles: Splinter and shard

Names: Keating, Lulu, author.

Identifiers: Canadiana (print) 20230580688 | Canadiana (ebook) 20230580718

ISBN 978-1-77041-745-8 (softcover)
ISBN 978-1-77852-274-1 (PDF)
ISBN 978-1-77852-273-4 (ePub)

Subjects: LCGFT: Short stories.

Classification: LCC PS8621.E23475 S65 2024 | DDC C813/.6—dc23

This book is funded in part by the Government of Canada. *Ce livre est financé en partie par le gouvernement du Canada.* We acknowledge the support of the Canada Council for the Arts. *Nous remercions le Conseil des arts du Canada de son soutien.* We acknowledge the funding support of the Ontario Arts Council (OAC), an agency of the Government of Ontario. We also acknowledge the support of the Government of Ontario through the Ontario Book Publishing Tax Credit, and through Ontario Creates.

ONTARIO ARTS COUNCIL
CONSEIL DES ARTS DE L'ONTARIO
an Ontario government agency
un organisme du gouvernement de l'Ontario

Canada Council for the Arts | Conseil des arts du Canada

PRINTED AND BOUND IN CANADA

PRINTING: FRIESENS 5 4 3 2 1

CONTENTS

MOTHER LODE

Polly so rarely had visitors that when she heard the thump of their heavy boots on the outside stairs, she ran to the door and pulled it open. Two RCMP officers, in uniform. On the street below, she saw the cruiser parked in front of the bakery. Polly's hand flew up to her hair. She'd brushed it a hundred times that morning and piled it loosely on top of her head. Her dress was a cotton print, plain but clean. Her nylons didn't have holes in them. They asked if they could come in. "Yes, of course."

There were only two chairs in the tiny sitting room, so she invited them into the kitchen. With nothing to do but keep house, the dishes were done and the kitchen was clean. She whisked the *Ladies' Home Journal* off the table and put it face down on the counter. The March 1965 issue — only a few months old. Yesterday she'd been to see the meddling old doctor. On her way out, she'd slipped the magazine under her sweater. Surely they weren't here about that? No, they would not have sent two Mounties about a magazine that cost thirty cents. She looked at the young one, tried to catch his eye, but he wouldn't look at her.

The officers sat across from her. The older one did the talking. He had a bushy moustache that needed a trim. He was asking her if she had anyone who could come to be with her. Polly realized now that he'd already asked her this at the door.

"Your mother? Mrs. Broderick lives over town, doesn't she?"

Now that she, Polly, was Mrs. Maurice Doucette, she did not want Mrs. Broderick. She shook her head.

"My mother is sick," she said.

So if they weren't here about her mother, that meant they were here about Maurice. Her mother disapproved of Maurice. At the wedding, when Polly should have been the centre of attention, her mother held her head high, peering down like a giraffe on Maurice's family. Never again would Polly allow her mother to stomp on her choices. If she invited her mother to be here with two officers of the law, she'd perform for them. No, this was Polly's moment, her performance.

She wanted the Baker from the shop downstairs to put his beefy arms around her. She could lean into his neck, sob into his chest. But that was out of the question. Besides, this was his busy time. Through the floorboards, she could usually hear the housewives' chatter. Why so subdued? Yes, they would be whispering about the cruiser outside, the two officers upstairs. More than ever, she hated the smell of fresh bread.

The bushy moustache was wiggling as he spoke. Now she could see the MacKinnon in him. She'd gone all through school with Vince, his son. Vince was a little shit, but he had a nice father. Polly remembered that he'd told her his name when she opened the door. But that was centuries ago, before the world had tilted, before she'd become an iceberg in the Arctic Ocean.

When Polly offered tea, both men nodded solemnly. Tea has been bringing comfort to Maritime kitchens since the 1500s. She rose from the table, suddenly cold. Polly heard thunder as a chunk of her broke away. She was an iceberg and she had calved. She felt chill spray as her man, Maurice, splashed into the Arctic waters. The ripples nudged her away from the table, up against the stove. She couldn't look behind, knowing that Maurice was floundering, bobbing in his ocean, melting, sinking. She picked up the kettle from the stove. Swirling icy currents carried her to the sink. Generations of Celts told her she must let the water run cold to make good tea. MacKinnon spoke again. He needed to know what she wanted. Polly couldn't get her head around what he meant. Rarely had she been asked what she wanted.

"The body?" he asked. "It can be shipped home if that's what you'd prefer. Or buried there, in the Yukon."

The young one glanced up at Polly. He was about her age, early twenties. She saw pity in his eyes, as if her life was over now and she was no more than a beached shipwreck. She was suddenly repulsed by his peach fuzz and persistent pimples. So what if he's a Mountie. She might only be a housewife, but there was more to her than met the eye. Icebergs keep seven-eighths of themselves hidden underwater. When she rallied — and she would — then watch out!

She set the teapot on the table, draped it with the cheery tea cozy she'd knit herself.

MacKinnon was persistent. "The detachment in Dawson City is keeping it frozen. They wants to know."

She was dizzy now and sat down with a clunk.

Polly's next thought: Why aren't I crying?

Tanner arrived at the edge of the glacier. Ice stretched all the way across the valley to the distant mountains. It glittered so brightly his eyes were forced almost shut. The glacier, a living moving beast, oozed out of the far mountain plateau. It crept forever forward, inch by inch, a restless, ruthless stalker. Boulders as big as houses were rolled along like pebbles. Blue cracks split the ice from surface to bottom. The crevasses reminded him of stretch marks on a pregnant woman's belly, like he'd seen on Elizabeth in Saskatchewan. Back then, they were wrapped inside a sweet cocoon, blissful and chosen, as if no other humans had ever created a baby. That was before it all went wrong.

Strange that it was this glacier he'd thought about, not the creek. All through the fall, throughout the dark winter and during spring breakup, this icefield lay inside his head, a constant cold stab just back of his eyes.

Late last summer, Tanner had crossed the glacier to the mountains on the far side. As the map had promised, he'd found a creek trickling down from those lazy mountains. Because he'd promised Elizabeth he'd be there for the birth, he had ended up with only one day of panning. There was fine grey gravel in that creek, ground down by the millstone of other rocks. He had found the sparkle of gold — just colours, but who's to say there weren't nuggets there too. Now, finally, he was back, and the dream of finding gold would become a reality.

A percussive noise echoed off the mountains. Turning, Tanner saw that Maurice had his hatchet out and was chopping down a tree. What the hell?

The tree was a skinny black spruce, just three inches at the base, the same height as Maurice (and Maurice was not tall). How could it be a hundred years old? That's what he'd heard about these high-altitude trees, but he didn't really believe it. Tonight, he'd count the rings. He felt sorry for taking it, but he needed a pole now that they had reached the glacier.

It had been a hard slog up from the river. Tundra, he discovered, is deceptively difficult to walk on. When he had appraised the long slope that stretched up for miles, Maurice had thought it would be an easy hike. There was only low brush. The trees were sparse, so there would be no bushwhacking. But as he discovered, you don't walk on tundra: you walk in it. The forward boot sinks into the soggy moss and swallows your foot. Water closes in over it. Then you have to yank hard on the back boot to break the suction. Miles of this. His thighs ached from the effort. He should have cut the damn hiking pole at the start of the climb.

The moment Tanner had mentioned gold, Maurice knew he wanted to join him prospecting in the Yukon. They'd met in a New Brunswick logging camp, back in September, and planned to join up in the north in late spring. Maurice had a feeling that he was on the brink of something monumental. When he'd raved about it to Polly, she said he was always unrealistically optimistic at the outset, then inevitably disappointed. That's why, she said, after three years they were still living in an apartment. But Maurice knew that this time was different. He had butterflies in his stomach as the trip drew closer, and he took this to be a sign that his luck was changing. He was smitten with gold fever even before he'd dipped a pan in the creek.

In late May, Maurice and Tanner met up in Dawson City in a tavern called the Pit. It was noisy and smoky and crowded with people of every age, in various stages of dress and undress. As Maurice walked past tables with bearded men hunched over beers, he was grateful that Tanner had chosen bar stools at the far end of the tavern, away from the stink of them. Two young women flitted in and out like swallows, but Maurice sent them away, explaining that they were both married men. Maurice wouldn't let loose women steer them off-track, even though he knew that his and Tanner's marriages were both in trouble. Perhaps he could save his — if they found the mother lode.

Tanner ripped a sheet out of a newspaper. With a flat carpenter's pencil, he drew the map: the river they'd paddle, the clearing in the bank where they'd pull out, the old trail they'd follow up, up through the tundra. On the far right edge of the newsprint, he sketched a jagged line that was the mountain range. A wiggly line at the base was the creek.

Maurice pointed to the gap between the tundra and the faraway creek.

"What's in here?" he asked.

"After the tundra? This big honkin' glacier," Tanner said. With the flat side of the pencil, he shaded in the area.

Tanner had neglected to mention the glacier. Maurice was intrigued; he'd never seen one. He grinned, excited about all the new experiences — first time in the north, first summer without dark, first time panning for gold.

That night, in the shabby room they shared above the tavern, Maurice had the dream. He'd felt the cold, as solid as a wall, pressing in. The chill was all around him, until he became the chill. His moaning and groaning woke Tanner. For his roommate's sake, Maurice made light of it. But long after Tanner was snoring again, he was still awake. His grandmamma had dreams that came to her as warnings, and her stories had scared him as a child. The rising sun slowly brightened the shabby room. Maurice was relieved to find that it was only four a.m. A long day of packing and canoeing lay ahead, and he needed to get back to sleep. He convinced himself that the dream was nothing. Nothing that required a man to write a letter to his wife, though he got out of bed and did just that.

They were picking up supplies at the Trading Post when Maurice spotted the crampons. The map told him there was a lot of glacier to cross, but when Tanner saw the price tag, he shook his head.

"Nah. All we need is chain and wire," he said. "We'll find a length of chain, make our own."

Maurice was discovering that Tanner wasn't just a fancy dresser. He had no end of know-how and skills. The man was always reading, taking notes, making things. If he said they could use chain and wire to make something that would grip the ice, Maurice believed him. He'd never met anyone as smart and handy as Tanner.

They forgot to check the dump for a length of chain. Before launching the canoe, Maurice remembered the crampons and suggested, "Let's buy 'em."

Tanner said, "There's another solution. don't fall."

Maurice whistled as he limbed the tree. Back east when he was driving logs on swollen rivers, a pole was an essential tool. A pike pole held horizontal gave balance; held vertical, it was a third leg. Maurice refused to be spooked by his nightmare, but still he didn't want to risk an injury. They were many days from the nearest help.

Tanner heard whistling behind him. Twisting around, he saw that Maurice was trimming the branches. The whistling was a relief from the endless talking. Tanner had forgotten how much Maurice had chattered in the logging camp; somehow, with the other men around, it hadn't seemed so bad. He hoped to God his companion would run out of noises to make soon. Ahead of them lay four months of living together. He'd heard a story a few years back — two men going in and only one coming out. Chainsaw Charlie reported that his partner got lost in the bush. Then some Tlingit hunters found his partner's body with the head bashed in.

Tanner felt the weight of the sky, a deep blue pressing down on him, heavier than the forty-pound pack on his back. Not a cloud broke the intense glare of the sun. He took a deep breath of the cool air rising off the glacier, and it was like sucking an icicle. Since they were taking a break, he might as well get comfortable.

He wiggled his shoulders out of the leather straps, and his knapsack fell to the ground. Crossing his arms and reaching down, he whipped his shirt up over his head. He yanked open the snaps on the leather pouch on his belt, releasing his hatchet. The weight of it felt right in his hand. Balanced, a good design. With a well-placed swing, the hatchet sliced a wedge of ice from the glacier. The chunk was the perfect size. He rubbed the ice across his sweaty chest. Only when he'd raised goosebumps did he swing it around to cool his back.

He gazed ahead. Almost there! They'd be able to cross the glacier in a few hours. If they were lucky, they might find gold that very day. It wasn't like they were going to run out of light.

He could see now that Maurice was making a pole. Well, Tanner didn't need a pole because his boots had good grips. They were the best boots money could buy. Made of fine leather, they laced halfway up his calf and glowed golden against the vivid greens of the moss. First thing in the morning, dubbin stinks to high heaven, but he always slathered it on thick so his boots wouldn't leak. He wiggled his toes. No blisters, so that was good too.

Tanner shouldered his pack, shirtless, and commanded his weary thigh to lift his foot out of the tundra. As the suction broke, the sound was like pulling a cork from a bottle. He flung it up twelve inches, planted the boot on the tongue of ice. Leaning forward, he extricated his other boot, hauled it up, and then he was standing tall on the ice. As he flung his shirt over his shoulder, he stepped forward boldly. His front foot slipped. He shifted his weight to the back foot. It slid to the side. He let go of his shirt as his arms windmilled. His legs flew up and he fell, hard, and the air came out of him as a groan and then a curse.

"Damnation!"

Polly watched Officer MacKinnon twirl his wedding ring. The fingers of his right hand turned it around and around. It was as if he meant to twist it on so tight that his wife would stay put, would never leave, never die. She gazed down at her own wedding band, peeking out from behind the flashy diamond engagement ring. Maurice had romanced her with glittering promises. Who was the bigger fool, Maurice with his extravagant fantasies or Polly with her misplaced faith?

They sipped the tea. She hoped the men didn't mind that she served it black. Since she didn't take milk anymore, there was none in the house. The sugar bowl was on the table, but no one reached for it.

MacKinnon told her again, about the accident. This time she was surprised to hear him say "crevasse."

"The Arctic Ocean?" she asked. She heard the pleading in her voice.

"No. They weren't anywhere close. The ocean'd be a thousand miles away, give or take. The crevasse is on a glacier, see? A glacier, in the interior of the Yukon."

A crevasse? Isn't that a crack? Polly shook her head. She could be an iceberg in the ocean, but she could not be a crack in the ice. Polly twisted the engagement ring — always too tight — until it released its hold. When she tilted her hand down, the wedding band — always too loose — clunked onto the table.

There was no point getting the bank book from the drawer beside the stove. She knew what their savings were. She should never have let Maurice talk her into quitting her job. She liked the Five to Dollar. The fabric department had been her empire, and she oversaw stocking it with everything from tailor's chalk to seam rippers.

She put the rings beside each other. The eyes of the Mounties were on her, but she felt no need to explain. Would Cameron's Jewellery buy back Maurice's promises?

Maurice heard the grunt, then the curse. He looked: Tanner, flat out on the ice. Maurice grabbed his pack and his pole. He raced to the edge of the glacier and planted the pole firmly in an indentation on the ice. Then, cautiously, he stepped up onto the glacier.

A tall man like Tanner, with a heavy pack, fell hard. Maurice, broad shouldered and short, was more grounded. He stood over his motionless companion and wondered if he was dead. He tapped Tanner with his pole. Tanner rolled over, rubbing his back and then his hip.

Maurice's relief was out of proportion. In the chest pocket of his jacket, on the heart side, his letter was hidden away. The single word on the sealed envelope, *Polly*, now seemed overly dramatic. The dream meant a tumble, nothing more serious than that, and it had happened to the arrogant dandy, not him. It was, as his grandmamma used to say, "a fart in a mitten." The letter wasn't necessary. He'd burn it in tonight's campfire.

Maurice laughed and thumped his chest. "'Don't fall.' Dat's what you tells me, Tanner." When Tanner looked up, Maurice laughed even louder.

Using his pole to anchor him, Maurice jumped into the air. He clicked his heels. He danced as lightly as a ballerina, leaping and landing as if he were on solid barn planks. He sang at the top of his lungs.

For he goes birling down, a-down the white water;

That's where the log driver learns to step lightly.

Maurice danced in a circle around Tanner, the sluice pan, hanging from his pack, banging up and down against his thick thigh like a tambourine.

It's birling down, a-down white water;

A log driver's waltz pleases girls completely.

Tanner rolled over onto his front. He planted both his fists firmly on the ice and cautiously pushed himself up. He brushed the meltwater off his chest and pulled his shirt back on. Then Tanner carefully picked his way across the ice. Maurice, still singing, danced along behind him.

Maurice saw all this, Polly thought, her head bobbing toward the train's window. Oceans of trees all across the country, from the forests of the east to wherever they were in western Ontario. Maurice would be itching to be out there among those trees, pruning shears in hand. He'd snip off the bottom branches and trim the tips to shape them into Christmas trees. She was in the wilderness of Canada's vast interior, and it made her inconsolably lonely.

Polly reminded herself why she was here. The cost of transporting the body back home was prohibitive. It was cheaper to bury Maurice up north, and she felt she had to attend the burial because she had loved him and she loved his family. The Doucettes were Acadian, a chattering horde of brothers and sisters and cousins, aunts and uncles and parents. They held a riotous wake without the body at the old homestead, where Maurice's mother told Polly that she would always be her daughter. Everyone had hugged her like she was one of them. But nobody offered to accompany her. They all had their own families to look after. Maurice was her husband so they left it to her.

The last time they were together, Maurice and Polly had fought about Christmas trees. It was their first real fight in three years of marriage, though Polly had come to feel that all she did was wait for him in the apartment above the bakery. He'd returned from the spring seal hunt with only one day before he left for his trip north. They'd had sex and were lying in bed in the middle of the afternoon. He had handed her the lipstick from the bedside table. Dutifully she'd applied it again. He never tired of watching the way she held the lipstick steady and slid her lips back and forth across it.

He got talking about the house he would buy with a woodlot of spruce and fir, maybe even a few pine. Christmas trees would be his shoulder-season industry, shaping the trees in the spring, chopping them down in the fall. Polly had heard it all before. She thought about the grimy dollars he'd handed over. Could she have miscounted? Such a puny amount, but after his travel and expenses, there was never much left. Their savings were hardly growing at all. She had brought it up again, pleading that he let her go back to work.

Maurice said, "Nobody will see my wife out der workin'."

"But we don't have enough to buy an outhouse," Polly said. "We'll both have white hair before we can afford a house with a woodlot."

Maurice promised to let her work in the tree business. He'd teach her how to wrap the trees with baling cord for shipping to the Boston States. Polly asked how he planned to transport the trees. They'd need a truck; they didn't even have a car. (The one he'd used to court her was still up on blocks behind the bakery.)

It was the first time she had questioned his plans. And it was the first time he'd yelled at her. Wasn't he working hard enough as a lumberjack, a stevedore, a hunting guide? He listed the things he killed — fish, game, lobsters, and crabs. Hadn't he just spent two months on the ice, clubbing seals? He did this for her, and all she did was complain. Polly answered that she wasn't complaining; she was being realistic.

Listening to Maurice rant, she finally understood that she'd married someone with big dreams who was incapable of translating them into reality. Most painful was acknowledging that her mother had been right about him.

For a man who talked so much, Maurice was obstinately silent after their fight, and Polly didn't even try to patch things up. She was nostalgic for their early days. At the ceilidh where they'd met, he had a reputation for being the best dancer. He danced her all the way from the community hall to the river, where he'd shoved a log into the black water and leaped onto it. She watched him spin and dance that log into the current. This is the man I will marry, she'd decided, and she lost sight of him. She heard a shout followed by a splash. He startled her, showing up out of the dark, dripping and shivering. Polly took him home and built a fire to warm him up.

For a long time, their fire burned hot. Maurice went away to work, and when he returned, Polly stirred the coals, getting oxygen to the embers. Lately she couldn't raise much heat.

While Polly's husband gave her too little attention, the Baker was smothering her. With his hands as big as oven mitts, he kneaded her breasts and her buttocks. In the middle of the night, when he left to make bread, he tucked a quilt around her as if she was a lump of dough. Polly rose with the warmth so that when he returned for that special hour before he opened the shop, she was ready to be nibbled and poked and consumed. Lately, though, she was feeling eaten away, diminished. The smell of the baking bread wafting up through the floorboards made her nauseated.

The morning after their fight, Maurice snuck away without waking her. Polly did the same when she left on the train for the north — she didn't say goodbye to the Baker.

The map on her lap swayed with the motion of the train. She knew more of her country now, some of Canada's cities, their train stations with their dusty waiting rooms and wooden benches: Montreal, Toronto, Thunder Bay. Winnipeg would be next. She was booked on C.N. as far as Edmonton, then a bus to Whitehorse, and after that she wasn't sure how she'd get to Dawson City. The woman who had booked her ticket offered to make a long-distance call at Polly's expense, but she'd decided she couldn't afford the call. Her map showed a road from Whitehorse to Dawson, most of it gravel. She'd read that the journey took at least eight hours. Had she made the wrong decision? But what other decision could she have made?

Polly looked past her reflection, out at the darkening landscape. The trees blurred as the train thundered past, and she heard the mighty ones fall. They all toppled — the Mounties, the townies back home. The Baker, a rounded maple tree, suctioned into a twirling back wind, was twisted off its trunk. Her mother, a spar tree taller than the others, went down with a mighty crash. Well, there's no turning back, she thought: a twenty-two-year-old widow, her future dim and her savings diminishing.

The slippery glacier kept rising before them, making the ascent treacherous. Tanner ploughed on, one careful foot after another. He glanced back. Maurice had ceased his reckless dancing and singing and was following, his pole supporting him like an oversized cane. That night in Dawson, Maurice had woken him with his loud groaning. No wonder the man had bad dreams with the jobs he did. Tanner could never club seals — all day on ice floes, jumping from one to the other. His nightmare: he was on a stretch of Saskatchewan wilderness that he dimly recognized. He reached down to pick up the surveying rod, and his eye spotted the new highway. He saw that it was ramped too steep on the curve. There was an eerie silence, the road waiting for the fatal crash.

Elizabeth claimed it wasn't Tanner's fault. It was the engineer who designed the highway. Since he quit being a surveyor, the uninvited dreams weren't as frequent. He hoped they visited the engineer too.

Tanner resolved that when they made camp by the creek, he'd pitch his tent far away from Maurice's. There was no need for both to be hounded by each other's fear.

Maurice was talking about log driving. Three generations — it was in his blood. He had lost an uncle who slipped off a spinning log and fell under a boom. The men, leaping from log to log, had tracked him as the current pulled him along under the timber — his fingers poking up and once his chin, mouth open, sucking air. But then they lost him for good and found him two days later, wedged in a jam. They'd already planted the explosives, were about to blow it sky high, when they saw his boot.

Tanner had heard the story before. He stopped listening so he could reflect on his recent discoveries about light. The *Farmers' Almanac* had led him to library books that furthered his understanding. Night was disappearing by increments of twelve minutes a day. At this point in May, there was no more astronomical twilight. By early June, there would be no nautical twilight — no dark at all. Morning birds would chirp around the clock. No stars, the moon a pale ghost in a bright sky. Light would push in on his tent, making the canvas glow through the witching hours. He'd tie his bandana across his eyes, as he had done last summer. Like a burlesque dancer slowly removing veils, the north was gradually exposing her surprising marvels. Sometimes the titillation became too much for Tanner. He craved the predictability of the seasons he'd grown up in. Yet he also longed to stay year-round to experience all the north's seasons, to shed the Cheechako label and earn the status of Sourdough.

Tanner didn't get home in time for the birth, even though he'd left in time. The baby came a month early. It was nobody's fault, but Elizabeth blamed him for not being with her. She blamed him for making her pregnant in the first place. How had she transitioned from ecstatic to so utterly miserable?

Over coffee, Elizabeth's mother told him about the birth. She spoke in a low voice, like a priest breaking an oath of secrecy. She said Elizabeth had endured intolerable pain for two and a half days before they did the Caesarean. Then the infection set in, and she developed a raging fever. All the while, baby Samuel was in an incubator. When Elizabeth had recovered enough to come home, she didn't care about the baby. It was Tanner who held him, gave him bottles, and marvelled at his tiny extremities. He discovered that the baby had the same fold in his right earlobe that he had. He was thunderstruck.

The glacier levelled off, and Tanner was thankful because the walking was easier. He was suddenly stopped by a yawning crevasse. A smell wafted up from the ancient ice, the woes of hundreds of years of snow, trapped and compressed. He could, perhaps, leap across, but his heavy pack made him unstable. That early tumble had enforced a healthy respect for the ice. He looked to the west, but the split widened; to the east, it narrowed. When he diverted east twenty feet, he recognized the spot where he'd crossed last year, where he could comfortably hop across.

At first, they called Elizabeth's condition "baby blues," not uncommon in new mothers. But months went by and Elizabeth never came back to her right mind. The doctor diagnosed her as neurotic and prescribed electroshock treatment at the mental institute. Nobody wanted that.

Elizabeth's mother took her and the baby in. There was no place for Tanner. And there were medical bills to be paid. He'd never been to the Maritimes, never worked as a lumberjack, but he needed something radically different. He quit surveying for good, grateful that Elizabeth was too ill to protest his decision. He left his wife and son with assurances that if there was a change, Elizabeth's mother would send a letter.

Before heading to the Maritimes, Tanner had dropped down to Swift Current to visit his father. He talked the old man into letting him trim his hair. When he saw the same fold in the earlobe, he fell apart and confessed to his father: he despaired that the woman he loved would never come back from her dark place. His father simply advised, "Keep the faith, son."

Tanner heard a rapid whooshing noise behind him. Then another, and Tanner realized it was above him. Wings. A low-flying raven swooped down in front of him, then wheeled off into the sun.

In the wake of the bird, Tanner heard the silence. There was no noise from Maurice, no endless jabbering. He didn't want to turn around. But he did, slowly.

The white ice with its blue veins stretched back to the green tundra. To the east and west, there was not one object to break the monotony. The glacier was bare.

Tanner raced back to the crevasse, not to where he'd crossed but where he would have jumped if he was an overconfident log driver. He threw himself down beside Maurice's pole and peered into the fissure.

The gap was three feet wide at the top and narrowed as it went down. And there, far below, was Maurice, wedged in tight. Tanner yelled down, but there was no reply. He wondered if Maurice was even alive. Then there was movement. As Maurice craned his head up, his hat fell off, sliding down the ice and disappearing into the void beneath. Even in the diminished light, Tanner could see the trapped man's eyes were open wide with fear.

Tanner yanked the ice pick from his pack. He unclipped the rope; it was twenty-five feet. His years of surveying made distances a quick read. He felt a rising dread that it was not long enough. He pounded the pick's sharp point into the ice as close to the edge of the crevasse as he dared. Then he tied the rope to the pick and tugged hard to make sure the knot would hold.

When he looked down again, Tanner saw Maurice flailing one arm, straining to free it from the backpack. But the icy walls on both sides pressed in like a vise grip.

Tanner called down, "I'm dropping the rope." He regretted that his voice warbled. He made it steady by adding loudly, "Get ready to catch it."

They both watched the rope fall, uncurling slowly. It ended short, several feet above Maurice. When Tanner saw the outstretched hand, the fingers opening and closing, he pulled back.

He turned away from the fissure and looked off toward the distant mountains and imagined the creek beneath it. There would be no prospecting now, no gold for Elizabeth. If only he'd bought thirty feet of rope.

Tanner felt the panic in him, plumping his muscles and poisoning his joints. He had to move. Without looking down, he pulled in the rope and coiled it. He dug a hole in the ice with the pick and wedged Maurice's pole into it. As he removed his bandana, Tanner yelled down that he was going for help. Rope, ladders, picks. A few men — experienced men. He tied the bandana near the top of the pole to make it easier to find the spot. They'd be travelling fast, perhaps in diminished light. How long would it take to get back? Tanner wanted to get away before Maurice asked. He didn't like the way it was adding up. When he got to the river, he'd have to line the canoe against the current, following the shoreline's curves, wading across creeks. It would take at least three days to get to Dawson, and despite how fast they travelled, another two for the return. As he calculated how much rope they'd need, Tanner found another reason to hate the surveying courses he took. A body at 98.6 degrees, in contact with ice, -32 degrees. Gravity . . . As Maurice's body heat melted the ice, he would descend further and further. They may not be able to get him out.

Maurice yelled up, "Letter." His breathing was forced, as if he couldn't get a complete lungful of air. Tanner saw him twist his arm around so that his fingers tapped his chest. Maurice sucked in air and said, "For my wife."

Tanner understood what was being asked of him: a letter was in Maurice's pocket. To give it to his wife, Tanner would have to retrieve the body.

They both knew he wouldn't live until Tanner got back.

"I will," Tanner promised. He slung his pack onto one shoulder. As he walked back along the crevasse, east, to where he'd crossed before, a familiar sound made him stop. Distant, strained — that tune again:

A log driver's waltz . . .

A pause.

. . . pleases girls completely.

Polly had spent so much time getting to Dawson City, she didn't care how rough the place looked. Nor did she care how rough she looked. She'd booked a cheap hotel on Front Street, right across from the confluence of the rivers. The first thing she did when she got to her room was pull off her nylons. It felt ludicrous to wear them here. She'd save them for the next day, for the interment. For today's meeting with Tanner, she wouldn't even bother with gloves or a hat. I've let myself go, she thought. But nobody was going to see her. Nobody who mattered.

The streets were unpaved, the air dusty. There weren't many people around. Dawson was a far cry from the photos she'd seen of the Gold Rush at the turn of the century. The old wooden buildings, if they weren't falling down, were propped up. As she stood looking at two old buildings that leaned into each other, a woman in a bush hat strode past her.

"The Kissing Buildings," she said. "Permafrost. Keeps shifting." The woman swung up into a derelict truck that was missing the driver's door. "Where're you from, honey?"

"New Brunswick."

Polly resented looking like she didn't belong and wondered how this woman knew she was from away. She didn't think the ancient truck would start, and when the engine wouldn't turn over, Polly felt vindicated.

"That's not too bad," the woman said as she swung down from the cab, adding, "New Brunswick. You'll fit in. You'll see."

Polly had no intention of fitting in. She watched the woman wrench up the hood.

"Here, honey, hold this for me, will ya?"

As she approached, Polly saw that the woman's face was scoured by the elements. She looked to be in her sixties. She poked some kind of lever. Polly figured it might be the starter. She wasn't sure about sticking her hand in, but the old woman wasn't shy; she took Polly's hand and placed it on the greasy lever. Polly thought, Good thing I didn't wear my gloves.

"Hold it," the woman said as she returned to the cab.

Polly saw a wire rise and descend repeatedly as gas was pumped. Then the engine roared to life. Polly pulled back, scared of her hand getting ground up.

The old woman steered with one hand as she shifted gears with the other. She abandoned the wheel to tip her hat at Polly as she pulled away. "See ya around, honey!"

It had been Tanner's idea to get together in person. She wished they didn't have to. A dog in a harness flashed past her, pulling a bicycle steered by a girl in her teens. When the dog veered toward a mangy mut, the girl shouted, "Go past!"

Polly watched the dog obey. At the intersection, the girl yelled again. "Gee . . . Come gee!"

The dog turned right, bicycle with girl following.

As she approached the hardware store, Polly was cut off by a hefty young woman striding out with a maul — not an axe, a maul. Maurice had taught her the difference. Seeing another woman working on an oil tank, the one with the maul raised it and charged, yelling. Her friend turned quickly and returned the threat, waving a large wrench. They exchanged a few friendly swings with their tools and laughed.

Polly envied them their blue jeans. She had packed only skirts and dresses. Maybe that was how the old woman figured she was new to town. Women here didn't wear skirts.

Swinging half doors aren't just in Western movies, Polly discovered as she entered the hotel tavern. A big dame — Polly recognized her from the bus to Dawson — brushed past. A tall barrel of a woman, she could easily be mistaken for a man with her red plaid hunting jacket and workboots. Hanging from her belt was an array of leather pouches, including a sheath holding a bowie knife. In a booming voice, she told the bartender — not asked but told him — that she was going to shower in the staff room. The water line from the creek to her cabin was clogged, she said.

"But you're not staff," he told her.

"No, and unless you let me clean up, I won't be," she said.

He tossed her the key. The bartender leaned toward Polly and said quietly, "Welcome to Dawson, where the women are men and the men are afraid of 'em."

Polly smirked. She'd only been in town a few hours and already she knew this. She was too self-conscious to ask for a vodka and orange juice, so she ordered a draft — these men-women probably drank beer. She found a seat facing the door.

She knew it was Tanner when she saw his silhouette in the doorway. Maurice had ridiculed him as a fancy dresser. She stood up, and as he approached her table, she took in his outfit — the bandana knotted loosely around his neck, the vest, the tall leather boots. He was handsome and healthy, and she immediately regretted making these observations.

The town was so turn-of-the-century, she felt that she should curtsy. They shook hands and sat down at the same time.

The bartender yelled, "The usual?"

"Yup."

"I got his pack," Tanner told her. "It's in my room. I'll bring it down. You want it now?"

There are many phases to processing a death, Polly realized. Moments ago she felt free of Maurice and now, suddenly, she was his widow. Her hands flew to her face, her fingers covering her mouth. She didn't trust herself to speak. She nodded.

Whiskey arrived in a shot glass. Of course, Polly thought, that's what he'd drink. Before the bartender left, Tanner downed it in one gulp and ordered another. When they were alone, he reached into his pocket and pulled out an envelope. Polly saw her name on it in faded pencil. She gave Tanner a questioning look. "He had it on him when he fell. Made me promise to get him out so you could have it. It was in his pocket —"

He would have said more, but Polly put up her hand to stop him. The paper made a crackling noise as she took the envelope. It had been wet, then dried. This envelope, Polly thought, had been soaked by the melting ice. A competition between the soft heat from Maurice's body and the cruel cold of the glacier. The glacier won. How long was the battle?

She looked up and was surprised to see guilt in Tanner's eyes.

She said, "He fell, right? He tried to leap and he fell. That's what the Mountie told me."

Tanner cleared his throat. "All I could think was to get help. I set off as soon as I knew I couldn't get him out. I should have stayed with him."

Polly wished there was something she could say to console the man, but there didn't seem to be any right words. She needed to read the letter that she held in both hands, afraid to open. It was her first contact with Maurice since he'd left.

Tanner stood. "I'll get the pack."

As soon as he left, his whiskey arrived. Polly felt that Maurice was the shot glass and he'd just joined the table. She was so sad that they'd parted on bad terms. Their last full day together, Maurice had done his husbandly act, and she had done her wifely duty. By then she knew that sex could be glorious ecstasy. She wondered if Maurice could have been taught what she'd learned from the Baker, without becoming suspicious. Probably not.

Maurice seemed pleased with her swollen breasts. It hurt her when he squeezed them, but she tried not to let him see. That's when she might have told him her suspicions. She couldn't face it yet. Then their argument, and Maurice's quick exit for the far north.

The letter was only one sheet.

"You've got this letter because I'm gone, pretty Polly," Maurice wrote. "I'm sorry. I figured out you're pregnant and I know it's not mine. It can't be mine, with the time I was away. I can count."

He made a joke: "I was angry. I needed to go north to cool off."

He gave her permission to choose the man she wanted. He hoped it wouldn't be the Baker. "I never liked his bread."

She folded the letter and put it back into its envelope. It bothered her that Maurice assumed she'd need another man to replace him. She had five months before the baby's birth.

At that moment, she decided she wouldn't tell the Baker about the baby. Nor would she return home to her mother. She wouldn't seduce the dandy. For the first time in her life, Polly was ready to be on her own. She didn't know who she was or what she wanted from life. But here, in this frontier town on the edge of nowhere, there was the possibility she might discover it.

When Tanner returned, she stood up. He watched her attentively as she pulled a few bills from her pocket to pay for the drinks.

"Where can I buy jeans?" she asked.

Tanner turned and pointed at the store across the street. While his back was turned, Polly drank his whiskey. She felt his eyes on her as she clunked the empty glass down. She took Maurice's pack from him and left.

THE MAKEUP MAN

Entering the kitchen, Shane is startled by the sudden flash of a face in the mirror on the table. He sees a tall man, his dark head silhouetted against the bright ceiling. Instinctively, Shane's hand flies up and wraps around his sunburnt face. He realizes he's seeing himself in the mirror, his own face, his hand. How can he be spooked by himself? It's too quiet here; he's too often alone.

Shane's curly hair is expertly styled. For the first time in his life, the cut is perfect (thanks to Katrina). It's greying now and that adds distinction. His skin, though weathered, is benefitting from moisturizers that Katrina makes sure he applies each night. He's wearing a designer T-shirt; Katrina's always getting top-of-the-line clothes at promotional events. Shane could be a model, except for the chest hair bristling out at the neckline. He's never looked so solidly handsome on the outside and felt so messed up on the inside. Who has he become? He used to say, without hesitation, "I'm a carpenter." Later on he boasted, "I'm a truck driver." Now who is he?

When it came to trucks, Shane knew how to take care of them. Except his last truck, now rusting in a junkyard, but when he bought the rig new in 2010, what a beauty! A Freightliner Cascadia, Daycab, 10 speed. He did the exterior maintenance himself. He'd pressure-steam the bugs out of the rad and hose down the running boards. He scrubbed the headlights with a toothbrush and toothpaste because some guy on the road told him it cleared the abrasion. Yep, he took care of the outside, but when it came to the engine, he trusted the shop across town. Let them run the diagnostics and do the work.

Shane, the person, is not as straightforward as a truck. The exterior is no problem: with Katrina's help, it's well taken care of. Now, the interior — if only there was a shop. He needs a recalibration, or a complete refit. The problem isn't the new marriage; that's running smooth. What's grinding the gears is that he's living in Florida without a green card. This move was Katrina's idea. This is where she wants to be. For now, he's living Katrina's dream.

Most of the problem is that he's homesick. The farther he travels and the older he gets, the more he feels the pull back to Nova Scotia. It's like his hair is woven into the old man's beard on the scrubby spruce trees. Shane's Irish ancestors planted themselves in Nova Scotia over 250 years ago. He's come to appreciate that whether he wants to or not, he's continuing their legacy. He greets strangers with a flick of the head to one side. He seals agreements with a handshake, not a lawyer. He shoulders grief quietly and supports others with the lightest touch. These things are in his bones. He is who his people are, and he'll never be anyone else.

He wasn't always gracious about this heritage. In his savage youth, he poured gallons of alcohol down his gullet to drown these roots. He's truer to his lineage than "them what's livin' up home." Now that he's in Florida, he longs for the taste of the salty winds off the Northumberland Strait, 3,500 kilometres away. He'd do anything to be back on those Atlantic shores assaulted by the smell of rotting kelp, instead of sweating in the humid heat that blows in off the Sargasso Sea. Makeup is strewn across the table. Before Katrina, Shane didn't have a clue about this stuff. Now he knows the lip liner, the eyelash curler, the contour brush. Tweezers are for eyebrow shaping, not for splinters. The perfume bottle. These are her tools.

The Professional Esthetician is a thick textbook feathered with Post-it Notes. It has become Shane's as much as Katrina's. Her ambition is to be an esthetician. That means passing the exam to get her certification. Her English has steadily improved since Shane brought her over from Russia, but the technical jargon in the textbook baffles her. Every day while Katrina is at work, Shane studies the textbook and learns the lessons. The drafting paper and notebook, the pens and pencils on the table are his. He makes drawings and graphs. Every night he teaches her.

He opens the textbook, flips to the last chapter, and wonders how to best teach electrolysis. Katrina resists having to learn it because most clinicians use laser hair removal these days, not electrolysis. But she'll be questioned about it on the exam. Tonight: electrolysis and review. Tomorrow night is the exam. The textbook is frustrating. There are not enough photographs and step-by-step illustrations. In the beginning, he made notes. Then he started making pencil sketches. Then he needed colour because how can you teach lip liner or eyeshadow without colour? At the mall's department store, he's come to appreciate the Korean salesman who helped him pick out pastels and later coloured pencils. The salesman thinks that Shane is a fellow artist.

Shane rubs his hand over his chin. All day long the prickly stubble bugs him, but Katrina has sensitive skin, so he waits until late afternoon to shower and shave. When she gets home from work, they usually fool around a bit. There seems to be no end to their mutual need to touch, and he doesn't want to give her beard burn. After dinner, he'd like to cuddle some more. There's no denying Katrina is ambitious. Without fail, she diverts his advances, clears the dishes off the table, and opens the book. He admires that about her. On her feet all day, coaxing big women into skinny jeans. But she won't let her dream die.

Could electrolysis take care of my chin? he wonders. It would be a long process to kill the beard of a fifty-year-old man. Not that he'd want to lose his beard, but he wonders about trans people, the guys turning into girls? He stops himself and examines the concept: it's not like that. Having a sex change is not simply beginning a new chapter — it's a whole new book. It's about claiming the sex you are meant to be.

Shane has learned this from Big Al, his trucking buddy. They had been on a long haul together and stopped for dinner. The florescent lights in the truck stop were too bright, but the booth offered privacy. Big Al asked if he could talk about trouble at home. Of course Shane said yes. After all, Big Al had helped him when his life unravelled. After Tammy kicked him out, Shane had rented a room at the Shady Grove Motel. For a whole bitter year, he went over the breakup again and again in his head. He couldn't seem to move on. In his younger days, he had a comfortable solution: he would invent his version of events and rehearse it until it was set, like concrete. He knew, and perhaps the new girlfriends did, too, that his sob story was fictional. Tammy's dreadful accusations kept thundering in his brain, and he wondered if she'd got it right. He needed to talk to someone, and it sure wasn't going to be some expensive shrink. Nor was he falling back on his old trick, a new girlfriend who'd buy his story.

Big Al just listened. Over many months of meeting along the highway, it all got said.

Shane saw the chain of events that led to the breakup. The Freightliner was a key component. Everyone had advised him to buy second-hand, but he went ahead and bought a brand new one. His payments were too high, and the recession meant he wasn't picking up enough loads. The financial pressure unsettled Tammy, and her bitching drove him away. No, that wasn't fair. Instead of doing something to reassure Tammy, he drank and partied and, regrettably, took comfort with other women. He was destructive. Tammy was not at fault. Shane hoped she'd accept his apology someday.

When Big Al got going about his family problems, Shane didn't want to hear about it, but he owed his buddy. There were already two little girls in the family, and when his son came along, Big Al had big dreams. All the stuff he'd do with a boy — fishing and trucks, mechanical stuff, man stuff. Then Big Al hung his head. He knew dick about dick. Tim had identified as a girl ever since he was two years old. Big Al didn't know how to love his son now that his son wanted to be his daughter.

Shane said he was there to help however he could. For years, he listened to Big Al talk stuff through. Just last week his friend had phoned with the news that Tim/Tina, who is now a young adult, is making arrangements for a sex change. What's the word Big Al used? Transition. Shane flips through the textbook's section on electrolysis. It's all about women's unwanted hair: face, crotch. Nothing about men who are transitioning. Katrina is right: definitely outdated.

The textbook photos of glamorous women bring him back to those tortured days in high school. He was so horny it was an illness. There was no room in his brain for algebra and calculus. His uncle kept waving the carpentry job under his nose. He took the paycheque to buy a car to impress the girls. Whenever someone slapped money in his hand, he stood taller.

Poor Katrina has to constantly reassure him that his contribution is just as valuable as hers. He's not convinced. As his savings dwindle, he feels a dark presence emerging, like the monster he always knew was under the bed.

Shane's cell rings. An unknown number. It's Arlo, from his truck-driving past in Nova Scotia. It's been a lot of years since they trucked together, but you can't shake someone like Arlo. Even if you never think of him, Arlo always considers you his best friend.

"For real?" Shane says. "You're in Daytona Beach? Let's get together."

"I'm in your hood, man! Now!"

"Well, okay, Arlo! Let's grab a coffee."

Shane moves toward the door, grabs his ball cap. He's in the habit of wearing a hat here. With his Celtic fairness and the beginnings of a bald spot, the hat is necessary.

"Fuck coffee!" Arlo yells. "I got somethin' better."

Shane realizes Arlo's gruff voice is in stereo, coming from the other side of the door and from his cell. A rap on the door. Shane pulls it open and there's Arlo, all six feet and three hundred pounds of him. The tee is stretched tight across the muscular shoulders; the belt is buried beneath the beer belly.

Arlo holds out a forty-ouncer of dark rum, then engulfs Shane in a tight hug.

Shane hates man hugs. When he played football, there was a lot of hugging and bum slapping, but that was in high school. There was also a lot of ragging about queers. As a result, he was afraid of contact with men outside of sports, afraid of being labelled a homo. He's thankful for his talks with Big Al. It's okay for men to be intimate, healthy even. Still, he's the one to break free of Arlo.

"Jesus — you're ripe!" Shane says. The stench of four days on the highway stings his nostrils. He beats his friend away with his cap.

Arlo steps past him and is inside, looking around the condo. "Wow! You're set up *real* good!"

Shane tries to quell the feeling of having been invaded.

"What's up? How come ya didn't let me know —"

Arlo interrupts. "They're loadin' my trailer tonight. I'm free till tomorrow."

Shane quickly pieces it together. Arlo has hauled a load from Canada, and they're refilling his rig. That highway-haunted look in his eyes means he's just pulled in. He hasn't slept.

Arlo goes to the kitchen and plunks the bottle on the table. He heads to the fridge, yanks it open. "Where's the mix?"

Shane hides *The Professional Esthetician* beneath oven mitts. He decides that he won't offer Arlo a place to crash. One drink and he'll send him off. Arlo closes the fridge and pulls open a cupboard. He pulls out a couple of glasses.

"So where are ya hidin' the little lady?"

"She's got a part-time job. She sells clothes."

"Ha, that works. You sponsor her, and she supports ya."

Shane is quick to explain. "Katrina came down here first, got the ball rolling, got into school, got papers. I'm still waiting."

Shane hears his voice, an edge sharp enough to slice the poor guy's ear off. Flashing back on all those parties over all the years, he remembers different women hanging off Arlo's arm. They were the same height (a head shorter than him), all blond and pretty and, ultimately, easily discarded. All the same except one. When Shane discovered that Arlo was romancing his sister, he took her aside and warned her: Arlo was not the kind of guy a girl got serious about. She was pissed off — it was none of her brother's business. Besides, who would take Arlo seriously? But she broke it off and that's what counted.

Settle down, Shane tells himself. Breathe. That was years ago.

"You got a special squeeze these days?" he asks.

"Ha! Don't ya hate that — when they miss their period and try to pin it on you? Why do ya think I took a long haul?"

Right. Shane nods. This shit again. His heart speeds up, and his stomach flips. He's learning to pay attention when his body has these reactions. Actually, it's Katrina who taught him this. On one of their first dates, they were in a bar. Some asshole singled out an underdog and started pounding him. Shane couldn't ignore it: before he gave it any thought, he was on his feet pulling the bully off. He beat the guy's face, even after he was down. And that was it. Katrina stormed out of the bar. He ran after her, and right there on the sidewalk she gave him an ultimatum. If he ever used his fists again, she'd find another way to immigrate. Someone else could sponsor her. Shane felt the ache in his fist, and another ache, even more fierce, in his chest.

His promise to Katrina is for himself as well as for her. He wants to change. So whenever he feels the rage coming on, he stops and tries to think it through. Here's Arlo, still a pimply teen when it comes to women. Still letting his dick point the way.

Shane is surprised to hear himself say, "Hungry? I can fix bacon and eggs."

Now where did that come from? How did he shift from being pissed off to offering to feed the guy?

Arlo emerges from the cupboard holding up a bottle of Coke. "Get a buzz on first," he says.

While Shane makes Arlo's breakfast, their banter is the familiar thrust and parry of the past. Arlo calls Shane a sissy for wanting too much mix in his rum. Shane teases Arlo about his unfinished house back home, still a basement bunker in the woods.

"A sight better than a condo in Florida," Arlo counters.

Shane claims they'll be moving back home before long. Katrina will soon have had enough of the heat. But in reality, there's no sign of her wanting to leave Florida's sun for Nova Scotia's fog. He thinks that eventually she'll see America's true colours. Canadians are less polarized about issues, more accepting of immigrants.

Shane puts the plate of bacon, eggs, and toast on the table. Arlo drains his glass and slams it down. He expects him to refill his glass. Shane suspects he could be wrong about Canadians.

After breakfast, on his third rum, Arlo brings up Big Al and wonders how he's doing. He brings up the "girly" son. Shane immediately springs into preaching mode, describing the kid's struggle with their gender identity and how hard it is on the family. As Shane hears himself go on, he realizes he's filling all the gaps so there's no room for any more slurs. But when he gets balled up in the *he*, *they*, *she* thing, Arlo laughs out loud at him.

"I'm just glad my private parts work," Arlo says. "And every woman I've ever shared my parts with agrees."

Shane wants to throw him out. Instead he tells him, "Hey buddy, feel free to take a shower."

That ends that.

It's no small task to translate complex text into everyday English, clear enough for Katrina to grasp and repeat on her exam. In the sketchbook, Shane fills a whole page with a drawing of a huge hair sticking above and below the skin. He's just finished printing the names of the parts when there's a roar from the living room.

"God damn them all, I was told we'd cruise the seas for American gold . . ."

Shane sees Arlo with a towel wrapped around his waist, strumming Katrina's long-handled back brush. He's got Katrina's pink shower cap perched on top of his wet hair.

He bellows, "We'd fire no guns, shed no tears . . ."

Arlo beckons with the brush for Shane to sing along, and he does.

"Now I'm a broken man on a Halifax pier, the last of Barrett's Privateers."

A great roar of raucous laughter from Arlo. He advances into the kitchen and picks up the perfume bottle. He points it at Shane. Squirt! Shane fans it away. Arlo ceremoniously taps Shane with the brush on one shoulder, then the other.

"You, Sir Shane, are a saint. You're livin' with a fuckin' princess. She got good stuff though," Arlo says, rubbing his bare arm against Shane's cheek. "I'm some smooth."

Shane jumps up from his chair. "Put her stuff back where you found it, Arlo."

Unperturbed, Arlo pours them each another stiff drink. "Hey, man, settle down. I get it."

Shane takes the offered glass, obliges his buddy by letting their glasses clink. Maybe, Shane thinks, I'm overreacting. I have to roll with the punches.

Arlo is returning to the bathroom when he says, "I checked out the Russian chicks on the dating site. They're not docile enough. Now them Filipino babes, they know how to service a man. Them Thai chicks too. But then I realized" — at the doorway to the bathroom, Arlo turns and flexes his bicep — "why buy a wife when you can get what you need for free."

Shane grabs something off the table. Three strides and he's within range of the bathroom door. He hurls it. Arlo jumps inside. Just before the object slams against the closed door, Shane sees it's the perfume bottle. It shatters, the glass falling and the liquid spraying onto the carpet. Arlo's laughter from behind the door makes Shane grateful he's not a fighter anymore, because he could murder this guy.

When he'd nuzzle Katrina's neck, Shane liked this scent. Never again. No amount of scrubbing could get the stench out of the carpet. All the windows are open and the AC is off. Arlo still hasn't come out of the bathroom. Shane figures he's waiting for him to calm down.

The kitchen's a mess. Maybe he should clean the dishes now. No, prepping for the exam is the priority. Shane has just sunk back into electrolysis when Arlo reappears. Dressed in his dirty clothes, the shower has done nothing for the stink. He toasts Shane and takes a long slug.

Shane takes a slug too. "There's something you should know about Russian woman," he says. "On the website, it says they're hard-working and ambitious. Katrina's that and more. Life's tough for women over there. She needs a hand up."

"You're helping her? Looks like she's the one helping you."

"She wants to be an esthetician." He can tell Arlo doesn't know what that means. "A beautician. Her dream job is to work at a spa, 'cause then she'll get better tips."

Shane holds up the hefty book. He's not sure if he can trust Arlo with this information, but the guy needs it spelled out for him. "Her English isn't good enough to process this. During the day when she's working, I study the textbook."

"So ya, like, explain it to her?"

"More than that. I translate it, so she can understand. See?"

He flips open the sketchbook and shows his step-by-step diagrams of braiding eyebrows, the numbered processes of facial massage. So far, Katrina has been the only person to see the drawings. Until now Shane didn't realize that he's proud of his work. He shows his most recent drawing of the hair, with sebum, follicle, and sebaceous gland identified in neat printing.

"Her exam is tomorrow night."

Arlo's eyes widen. "Oh my god! You're a makeup man!"

Arlo erupts in laughter. He slams the textbook with the flat of his hand. He collapses into a chair. He bends over, shrieking with laughter. Drool falls from his mouth to the kitchen floor.

Shane observes that he's actually seeing red. There's a rosy sheen to this scene playing out in front of him. What else is going on? Shane feels his heart pounding. His hands are curled up into tight fists. He can feel his fingernails cut his palms. The oath he swore to Katrina was that he'd never again use his fists.

A flat hand is not a fist.

Shane rises slowly to his feet and stands over the laughing man. He stretches out his fingers and places his hand on the back of Arlo's chair. When Arlo, still roaring with laughter, leans back to take a breath, Shane tips the chair. Arlo flings his arms out. Shane skitters out of reach. The chair crashes down. Arlo's head slams the tiled floor, bounces up, and slams down again.

Shane watches Arlo's mouth slacken and his eyelids slowly close.

"Well, that shut ya up."

"Hello?"

Katrina's distant voice wakes Shane. He opens his eyes and sees her standing in the entrance to the living room. She's well put together, he thinks. That leads to the next observation: I'm still drunk. I gotta be careful. He discovers he's sprawled across the armchair.

Arlo lies on the sofa, eyes closed, arms folded across his chest. Shane has a vague memory of dragging him here from the kitchen.

Katrina stays put in the doorway. Shane sees her glance behind her into the kitchen, where the chair still lies on the floor. On the table, the rum bottle is empty.

"What is happen?" she asks. She sniffs the perfumed air.

There's no fear in her voice. He likes that about her. Solid as a rock. A good mate when your ship is sinking.

Shane unfolds from the chair. The headache hits as soon as he's standing. He ignores it and crosses the room. He pokes

Arlo's shoulder several times before the man opens his eyes. Arlo rubs the back of his head.

"Say hello to the missus," Shane says.

Arlo looks around, trying to piece together the events that landed him here on the couch. Shane pokes him again, and he sees Katrina.

He mumbles, "Pleased to meet ya."

"Arlo. Truck driver," Shane explains as he hauls Arlo to his feet. "He's got to go back to his rig. Arlo, you need a taxi?"

Arlo shakes his head and winces. He fingers the back of his head again, finding the lump.

When Shane guides him toward the door, Katrina steps aside to make room for the two burly men.

"You found your way here. Guess you can find the way back, eh?"

When Shane opens the door, Arlo stumbles out. Shane and Katrina move into the doorway, where they stand side by side, watching Arlo weave down the hall.

"From back home," Shane says, hopeful that might buy him some slack. It does. Katrina calls out, "Next time, I cook you Russian dinner."

Arlo stops, turns around, and acknowledges with a jerky wave. Then he's gone through the exit. Shane looks at his wife. When she takes his hand and squeezes it, the thrill goes through him, all the way to the soles of his feet. So much is wrong: this condo, this country, the lack of a job, the absence of family and friends. His diversion into cosmetics is definitely weird. But somehow, he picked the right woman. He drapes his arm around his wife's shoulder and steers them back inside. This is very, very right.

"Sorry about that." He closes and locks the door.

She's already seen the mess and the empty bottle so he doesn't need to make excuses.

Not that she'd expect an explanation. She cuts him all the slack he needs.

"How about you relax for a bit." He gives her a peck on the cheek. "Dinner will be a little late."

PALE PONY EXPRESS

The little girl asks me for the story. Her blond ringlets hang to her shoulders. She's old enough to hear the truth. I want her to sit on my lap, but she tells me that seven is too grown up for that. When she's snuggled up beside me, I reel myself back, return to the woman I was before she took root.

It had been twenty days since we'd talked about it. Time was running out.

I suggested, "Let's take a run down to the Pale Pony." That's what we called Whitehorse.

Rory said, "We only got two days off. You wanna spend six hours each day drivin'?"

"Five," I told him, "if you let me behind the wheel."

He won't.

Even when you live off-grid, word gets around. The law of the north is that you can't refuse to help others. Sure enough, they came to us with their lists. Sandy needed a fan for his stove and a hard drive. Rebecca needed pasties for her burlesque. Sarah needed roofing nails. Really, Sarah? Your roof is under three feet of snow.

We were ready to go when Evelyn pulled in, blocking us. The bed of her pickup truck had a custom-built dog carrier. Three dogs stuck their heads out of round cubbyholes. Evelyn won't get to it right away. She introduced the dogs.

"Nobody will adopt them until they're fixed."

She'd go herself, but she's too busy at the shelter. "It's all lined up at the vet clinic."

She held out the truck keys.

There was only one cassette in the truck. After one hundred kilometres of Hank Snow, we shut it off. We finally talked about the stillborn (Gertrude). The doctor told us we were unlikely to lose another, but we saw death everywhere. The Klondike Highway was bruised with nightmare landmarks: where I slid off, where Rory crashed. Almost there, we skidded on black ice and bounced off a snowbank. When we finally arrived, we were grim and exhausted. After the errands were done, we agreed we would talk. My pregnancy. We would decide if we would go through it all again. It was still early enough.

The damn vet clinic ordered us back in four hours to pick up the dogs.

The pert assistant explained, "This is a freebie for the Dawson Shelter. You can't expect us to keep the dogs overnight."

Try sneaking three drugged-up cone heads into a pet-free motel. I distracted the desk clerk while Rory smuggled. The dogs kept us awake all night with their restless wandering. As soon as we fell into deep sleep, they needed out. That was the start of another nightmare day. The Malamute couldn't jump onto the truck bed. Rory lifted him: the dog twisted, nipped Rory, and ripped his stitches. Back to the vet.

By the time we made it home, Rory and I weren't talking. In bed, we kept away from each other. In the morning, Rory touched my belly. My hands covered his. Softening, clinging, crying. Tenderness reignited. We melted into each other.

"And that, little girl, is how you came to be."

PROMISSORY NOTE

Martha marvels at the dexterity of the nurse's efficient fingers as she places Lance's watch and wallet in a baggie and seals the plastic zipper. The nurse dangles the bag in front of Martha. She doesn't want to take it. She just wants the watch and wallet. Can't she have them without the bag? But it's too much trouble to ask. The plastic between her fingers squeals like corn starch and makes her nauseous.

As they head to the exit, Martha worries about what to do with the baggie. It's from a hospital, and what with the germs, she won't reuse it. It's a shame soft plastics can't be recycled. Or maybe they can? In some dim future, she sees herself looking it up online — checking the municipality's recycling regulations. Now, though, it seems like too much work.

Aloud, she says, "Oh, the hell with it."

"It's okay, Mom."

Martha hears her son's voice and realizes he's walking beside her. As the hospital doors slide apart, they're assaulted by the brilliant dawn, the low sun exploding over the parking lot. Martha stumbles, and Shamus tucks his arm around hers.

He's never been much for physical contact, but here he is, applying just the right amount of support. Shamus is a good son, grown up, responsible. She wonders why she still treats him like he's four years old and just wet his pants.

Movement at the far end of the parking lot catches her eye. It's a nurse. Then Martha realizes it's her nurse. The nurse who called her by her first name.

"Martha. Have a drink of water, Martha."

What's the nurse's name?

It's okay, Martha consoles herself, I'm not expected to remember. The nurse is unlocking her car. A twelve-hour shift and then more. She had promised to stay with Martha (and Lance) until everything was done. Done. What's that expression? Done and dusted. The expression they used? They "called it": Walter deceased at 6:11 a.m. Good thing Shamus was there. Maybe they waited for Shamus?

Of course. They had waited for Shamus.

Martha looks longingly across the parking lot. She wants her nurse to hold her again like she did outside the ICU. Ah, these stoic angels. Martha resolves to send her a card. Would Hallmark have one for the occasion? Thank You for Assisting with My Husband's Death.

"Come on, Mom. Get in the car."

Shamus is holding the door open for her.

Why the passenger door? It's my car, shouldn't I be driving?

She feels the impatient squeeze on her elbow. She looks at her son, so different from his father. She wants him to hold her the way her nurse did. Must she teach him this too? A car whooshes past, taking her nurse away.

"Mom?"

Shamus catches her when her knees buckle. He guides her into the seat. He bends low and lifts her legs, swings them in. Closes the door softly.

One tiresome task follows another. Pick out a suit, take it to the funeral home. Pick out a casket, snap at the funeral director. (What right has he, to be so old? Lance was only fifty-five.) As she storms out, she hears Shamus apologize.

The only calm is in the bedroom. Alone, curtains drawn, she clings to the blank where nothing happens. She lies on his side of the bed, imagines snuggling her husband. She stares at the lump on the bedside table that holds his watch, his wallet. She unzips the baggie, punishing it by shoving it to the floor where she'll stomp on it later. She can't help herself: she needs to explore his wallet.

Three twenties, one five, and a loonie. Sixty-six dollars. Isn't that the sign of the devil?

Martha shakes her head. *Don't lose it now.*

From downstairs: "Mom? We gotta go."

She's supposed to be dressing for the funeral.

Behind the auto club insurance, a slip of paper. Folded twice, old. In faded pen: "I.O.U. Good for one blow job — W."

She hears a distant car start. Shamus has started the car — her car.

Martha can only endure the endless funeral by scrolling through names that start with *W*. Her brain flips through office parties, summer barbecues, birthdays. She turns around to scan the attendees at the funeral. There's Wilma — she's seventy-eight. There's Wendy, but isn't she a lesbian? Shamus tugs her arm. She glares at him. He gives the smallest of nods, and she turns to face the front like everyone else.

In the receiving line after the funeral, she scans the mourners. All she cares about is each woman's first initial.

Hearing her sigh, Shamus says quietly, "The Griffins wish they could be here. They'll be back as soon as they can." The Griffins. Their best friends. A ripple of soft comfort bubbles through her. She resumes shaking hands with the Bs and hugging the Ts.

Since it was Shamus's idea to hold the reception at their house, she abandons him to carry it off. Martha sneaks into the study and closes the door. Lance's cellphone — *there must be some way to — yes!* The contacts are by first name. Wanda. Surely not Wanda Wong. Isn't she in Berlin now? All the other Ws are men. My god! Martha sinks into the chair. What if W is a man? Walter, Warren, William —

"Mom? People want to say goodbye."

In the attic, she frantically tears apart the cardboard boxes. *Who cares if I'm making a mess? Someone else can damn well clean it up.* Martha pulls out family heirlooms and tosses them on a heap. Finally she finds books at the bottom of the trunk, children's classics she couldn't bear to part with. One day Shamus will settle down. Not yet. He presents a new girlfriend every Thanksgiving, every Christmas, every Mother's Day dinner. Here it is! *Names for Your Baby*. She flips to the Ws.

Shamus's footsteps on the stairs. Why is he always sneaking up on her? The book is too big for her pocket.

"Mom? Stanley's waiting."

She hears herself say, "Oh, nothing" even though Shamus hasn't asked. Turning her back to him, she rips out the *W* pages — there are four for girls — and stuffs them in her pocket.

In the study, Stanley reads the will. Martha sits on her hands. It's all she can do to keep from pulling out the *W* pages.

What's Stan's wife's name? Amanda. Stanley finally gets to the "I bequeath" part. No surprises. Lance, ever the dutiful husband, left it all to her. Well, almost everything.

"I bequeath all my fishing gear to Tony Griffin."

Martha blurts out, "Tony and Gwendolyn!"

Stan explains, as if she's a child, "No, Martha. Not Gwendolyn. Just Tony. Lance willed his fishing gear to Tony."

Martha shudders. Gwendolyn. Tony calls her Winnie. Lance, too, apparently.

In the living room, Martha discovers she's standing in front of the mantlepiece gazing at the condolence cards that stand like soldiers on guard duty. What's the use of condolences? Aren't they really saying, "I'm sorry for your tragedy; glad it's not mine"?

Shamus yells from the kitchen in his business-as-usual voice. "The Griffins are back. Should I invite them over? We've got so much food — I can heat up the lasagna." Tony and Gwendolyn were down in Vancouver when it all happened. The day Lance died was the day of Tony's surgery.

Martha had resisted becoming friends with Gwendolyn. Just because the men worked together, why should she be expected to embrace the wife of her husband's colleague? Gwendolyn was the first to have a baby. Martha, pregnant with Shamus, was terrified about the pain that awaited her. She asked what it was like, giving birth. Gwendolyn said, "Like riding a jackhammer." And they laughed. When Martha's breast went hot and hard with mastitis, Gwendolyn was there with compresses three times a day. The women weathered motherhood together: the inoculations, the teething, the teenage years. They became closer than the men.

Far away, Shamus is talking on the phone. Before Martha realizes what she's doing, the condolence cards are in the fireplace, the flames shooting up the chimney. Shamus is suddenly beside her, his arms flapping helplessly by his sides. What can he do? What can anybody do?

"Mr. Griffin isn't up to it, but Mrs. Griffin is coming over."

"I don't want to see her," Martha says.

Shamus articulates as if she's inside that plastic baggie. "It's not their fault. He was already in surgery when it happened." As she heads for the bedroom, before she can slam the door, he argues, "She's your best friend, Mom!"

Later, when the doorbell rings, Martha simply goes into the bathroom and locks the door. She hears hushed whispering. Then, "Mom, I'm leaving to get some wine. Mrs. Griffin is here."

Gwendolyn stands outside, knocks, then tries the doorknob. "I brought flowers," she says in a sunny voice.

Martha scowls. The treachery, the betrayal. Her eyes fall on the towels that are stacked on the shelf perfectly, their rounded folds facing out. Inviting, like heated stones. Comforting, like hot compresses. She's grateful that Lance moved the linen closet from the hall to the bathroom.

She hears a distant car door slam shut. A car starts. Her car.

She hears, "Hello in there. It's me." A former best friend.

Martha turns the water on full. She squirts in too much bubble bath.

"Tony sends his love. He says he's so, so sorry. He cried, you know."

Once her clothes are off, she can't help looking at herself in the mirror. Lance wasn't her first lover. She wonders if he's her last. These are the breasts he cupped in his gentle hands, like this. Kissed. When she was breastfeeding, they wondered if it was true, that the strongest parts of an infant's body are the tongue and jaw. Does it take that much power to pull the milk out? Lance asked permission. She didn't say no. They discovered — they discovered together — how much sucking is necessary to draw out the rich milk. A moment so private between them, so intimate. Their secret.

She hears the deceitful voice starting in again.

"Open up, honey. It's just me."

Martha has heard this voice for twenty-five years. They whispered across the kitchen table while the kids napped. They balanced on stumps beside remote rivers while the men fished. They toasted with wine when their nests were finally empty and a lifetime of fresh liberty stretched out ahead of them.

Years ago, when she lay in bed with the fever, the mastitis, this voice stood in the doorway and whispered with Lance. Is that when he started calling her Winnie?

"Tony says — oh, how can I explain this? He wouldn't elaborate, just that it's related to the cancer."

Martha watches her foot disappear beneath the bubbles. The water is too hot. Her foot settles on the reassuringly solid bottom of the cast iron tub. They were right to keep this bathtub, even though it cost more to refinish than to buy some new acrylic thing.

"Tony gave something to Lance. Lance was meant to keep it for him until after the surgery. Actually, he said until he made a full recovery. Do you have any idea what he's on about?"

The next foot. It's burning her calves, but the pain is a healing balm. Gripping the edges, she lowers herself into the fire.

"Something to do with the prostate surgery and the treatment. He says it's my fault. He says I gave it to him when we were dating. He expects me to remember something from before we got married. Anyway, he wants it back. He says the doctors tell him he can use it soon."

Gwendolyn lowers her voice. Martha holds her breath so she can hear every word.

"Some slip of paper? You think you know a man; you think after twenty-five years . . ."

Martha stands up, gets out.

Gwendolyn pleads. "Come on, sweetie. Let's have a glass of wine, or two."

Martha, not bothering with the towel, unlocks the door, flings it open. Gwendolyn, with a bouquet of daisies, eyes one cluster of bubbles after another, trying not to see the private parts. Martha doesn't care. She throws herself at her friend, wraps her arms around her, and pulls her in so tightly the daisies are crushed between them.

ACROSS THE MOOSEHIDE SLIDE

Mandy clambers up into the cab. As she pumps the brakes, she retrieves the screwdriver, wedged against the brake pedal. Screwdriver into the ignition. Twist. Engine roars to life. She says, "And that's the right answer!"

It's eleven a.m. Mandy, still drunk from last night, flicks her head for me to join her.

I'm confused. We weren't supposed to drive anywhere. I'm all packed and ready for an overland hike. We're supposed to be climbing a trail, crossing the Moosehide Slide, and walking three kilometres to Mandy's cabin, north on the Yukon River where she's taking care of sixteen mushing dogs. After visiting a few days, I'll hike back alone.

I'm a teacher, I'm a mother, I'm fifty years old. I know better than to get into a vehicle with a drunk driver.

"Where are we headed?" I ask as I climb into the passenger seat.

Mandy slurs, "Glory bound."

I do something I don't do in Dawson City: I put on my seatbelt.

She says, "Next time I get paid, I'm gettin' insurance."

With each bounce through spring ruts, Mandy's long brown curls extend and retreat around her broad face. She's strong, stronger than any woman I know. She's also beautiful, and I guess in her late twenties. It's been a long winter for her. She says the routine is what drives you nuts: get up, feed the fire, eat, chop wood, feed the fire, eat, feed the dogs, feed the fire, sleep.

I used to live in a big boring southern city. After the last kid moved out, my husband did too. For a year, I kept teaching and kept house, waiting for him to come back. I shovelled snow all winter, mowed the lawn in the spring, raked leaves in the fall. I had a recurring dream of a body hanging from the big oak tree in front of the house. When I realized it was me, hung out to dry, I applied for the teaching position in the Yukon.

As I watch Mandy grind through the gears of her geriatric truck, it occurs to me that if I still lived down south, we'd never be friends. It was like this when I was a young teacher in Kenya. I discovered that isolation, whether geographic or cultural, makes for unusual companions. These friendships ignore education, religion, race, and age. The noose of social expectation is loosened.

Mandy pulls into the liquor store. While she's inside, I slide over into the driver's seat. When she discovers me behind the wheel, she tells me to pump the foot brake before releasing the emergency.

"Next time I get paid, I'm gettin' the brakes fixed."

The sled dogs, she says, are like a cast of characters in a play — the romantic male lead, the seductive female, the tragic hero, the jester. Her favourite dogs get an extra salmon or a bigger chunk of bear meat.

"It's day three for the dogs," she says.

According to Mandy, sled dogs can go three days without food. I've never heard anyone say that before. She shoves a cassette tape into the player and Johnny Cash belts out "Beans for Breakfast."

The truck bounces us back to the shed where Mandy stays when she's in Dawson. She calls it her "crash crib." Mandy has already killed her hangover with the first third of the bottle of Baileys. She offers me a shot. When I turn her down, she curses me for not drinking.

There's a hammock strung between birch trees. I float in the hammock, watching fresh new leaves on the birch trees quiver in time to the music coming from the truck, while Mandy packs her bag. She shouts along with Johnny: "And it burns, burns, burns, the ring of fire."

This time of year reminds me of my father. He went on binges. In the garage, he'd guzzle vodka for four or five days. Mom would sit with him to make sure he survived the rough ride down. I was sixteen when she refused to do it anymore. The vigil fell to me.

"Keep him sitting up," Mom said. "If he lies down and vomits, he might choke."

Even though I was studying for my final exams, I had no choice. I had to sit with Dad.

Mandy steps outside. She drains the last drop from the bottle, shoulders her pack, and heads off.

The trail up from Dawson is a steep climb through wooded slopes. Mandy's legs pound like piledrivers, wham, wham, wham. I flounder like a rubber Gumby. When it gets steep, she bounds up the slope like a mountain goat. She claims that if she were a hundred miles from town with a compass and a hatchet, any season of the year, she could make it back in good shape. I believe her.

We stand beside each other on the edge of the Moosehide Slide. Hundreds of years ago, the whole side of the mountain broke away and plunged into the river. Photographs of Dawson during the Gold Rush show the exposed face of the mountain, towering over the matchstick town.

Here in the north, nature doesn't pull its punches: the slide is treacherous. It's half a kilometre from one side to the other. The path is narrow and the shale is slippery underfoot. The steep slope is strewn with boulders the size of outhouses.

"Good thing it's dry," Mandy says, striding forward.

In no time, she's far in the lead and I lose sight of her behind an outcropping. When I round the obstruction, I see she's left the path. She's no longer moving forward but straight up the slope.

I yell, "Hey, Mandy! The path's down here!"

She keeps scrambling up the steep face. Loose rocks roll out from beneath her feet.

Now large stones are tumbling down in a loud avalanche. I take cover until it roars past me. Far below, the stones bounce onto the rocky bank and splash into the river.

Far up the vast slope, Mandy calls for me to join her.

I shout, "No! You come down here now!"

When she turns and looks at me, she suddenly realizes she's in trouble. Even from this distance, I can see she's swaying drunkenly. She clings to a boulder. She doesn't move, says she can't move. Turns out that Baileys is not a good travelling companion.

I could climb up to her, guide her down. But she's unpredictable — it would be dangerous for both of us. The other option is going for help. Getting to town and back would take at least an hour. Leaving her alone is out of the question. I plead with her. I tell her to walk diagonally across the slope, down to the trail. She stares back at me, says she won't move. Her flat blank face reminds me of the expression "rum dumb."

Years ago, in that other standoff, Dad sat rigidly in his rocking chair in the garage. He watched me while I studied my science textbook. It was exhausting, memorizing the periodic table and watching him guzzle, but that's what I had to do. Dad promised to take me out for a milkshake if I did well in the exam. And he promised he'd never drink again.

Far above me, Mandy whimpers. Suddenly I'm pissed off. I scream her name. I'm so angry I can see my command shoot up the slope. "Get down here *now*!"

Mandy lets go of the boulder. Sliding on her butt, she tumbles down. She curses as jagged rocks cut her. She uses her hands to keep from tipping over. Stones and clods of earth come with her. I shuffle along the path to where she's headed. I stand underneath, dodging the rockslide. When she slides close, I reach forward. I grab her and pull her to me. I punch her in the shoulder.

"What's bugging you?" she asks, indignant.

I yell, "You gotta stop this shit!"

She spits on her hands and rubs them against her legs. I see streaks of blood on her ripped jeans. She turns and continues across the slide. I watch her walk away. Mandy realizes I'm not following. She looks back at me briefly, turns, and hikes on. Her arm extends in a giant wave above her head, but she doesn't look back.

The night I was with my father, I fell asleep. I dreamed an earthquake was shaking the house. My mother was with me and we raced outside. We stopped in front of the garage and watched it crumble, the walls folding in. It fell out of sight into a deep crack. We walked over and looked down. There was my father's empty chair far below, making a scraping sound as it rocked back and forth. I woke to the noise of him choking. He was on the floor in a pool of vomit, gasping for air. By the time the ambulance arrived, my father wasn't making noise anymore.

Like a lot of the big incidents in life, Dad's death has never been discussed. Mandy and I are still friends, but we never talk about the hike across the slide. She still drinks. Me, too, but fear keeps my drinking in check. When the alcohol starts to have an effect, I feel a vibration not unlike an earthquake.

FORGIVENESS IN FOUR ACTS

Act 1 – Antigonish, Antigonish. Rotten Potatoes and Stinkin' Fish

The wood-panelled station wagon struggles up the hill to the cathedral. Bernice circles the building, seeking shelter from the glare of the sun. At the far end of the lot, she parks in the shadows. Here she can watch who comes and goes. Here she won't be seen.

She peers out at the stone-and-brick colossus that towers above the town. St. Ninian Cathedral was built two hundred years ago. It's solid enough to outlive the human race. Since annihilation is a definite possibility, the church might well survive after people are gone. The current threat is the Soviets, their missiles aimed at strategic points in the "free world." During the Cuban Missile Crisis, Bernice stockpiled canned goods in the basement. All the housewives were doing this, in Canada and the States. Long-range missiles are directed at bigger targets than Antigonish, Nova Scotia, so instead of a direct hit, they would die slowly of radiation sickness. Bernice decides that instead of them all huddling in their dark basements, she'll talk her friends into coming here with their canned beans. They can die more comfortably in the sanctuary or the choir loft.

Bernice's best friend, Marg, is married to a prof who teaches poli-sci. He says, and Marg repeats, that governments in the "free world" create these crises to drive people to consume more. What more could they possibly consume? Marg's pillow talk is world politics. That would not be pleasant, Bernice thinks. When I married Gordon, I made the right choice: a marine biologist. Over evening manhattans, early on, we discussed the surface cell structure of rockweed in the North Atlantic. After a while, Bernice didn't have to feign interest — she'd been seduced by biology. Later she'd read *Silent Spring* not to impress her husband, but because she was sincerely interested.

The day is bright, midsummer and full of promise. Since flying home all those weeks ago, she's been plagued by what happened in Vancouver. Bernice hopes that by entering the church, kneeling before the priest and making her confession, she will finally find peace.

Sitting in her car, Bernice rehearses, as if she's an actor in a play. She visualizes the confessional booth tucked into a quiet corner of the church There's the middle booth for the priest. He gets a door. The other booths on each side are for the penitents, and they only get a curtain. She'll push aside the curtain and enter the booth. She'll make sure the curtain is closed so nobody can see her inside. She'll kneel on the cushioned bench and bring her hands together, fingers pointing up. There will be no light. In the darkness, she'll become obsessed with trying to hear the voices from the other side of the wall, a mumbling that's not loud enough to make out. Then the dreaded noise, the thud as the tiny door on the other side shuts, and the squeal as the door beside her head slides open. It's the size of a picture frame. She won't be able to see the priest in his darkened cubicle, the screen obscures them both. But there's no anonymity. They will recognize each other. For seven years, Bernice served as president of the Catholic Women's League. She knows all the priests. She knows them too well. She hopes she'll get Father Fraser; he's kind.

Scene one — she has the first line: "Bless me, Father, for I have sinned." Then the words will tumble out of her mouth, her unthinkable sin. Scene two — having stated her sin, she must say she's sorry. This she does in the Act of Contrition prayer ("Oh my God, I am heartily sorry for having offended Thee . . ."). Scene three — the priest gives his forgiveness. And scene four — he assigns penance. She'll draw open the curtain and leave the confessional booth.

For a crime of this magnitude, the punishment (penance) will not be light. Maybe she'll have to attend Mass every day for a year. Whatever he assigns her, she feels the severity is unjustified. Bernice envisions yelling into the vacuous church, "I birthed eight Catholic children! I was a devoted wife. Does that count for nothing? Cut me some slack. Isn't life hard enough for a fifty-four-year-old widow?"

As Bernice sits in the station wagon gazing at the cathedral's unyielding stone, her eyes register movement. Two women are approaching. She knows them, of course, these shadow women, Theresa and Eloise. They look so old, bent with servitude, their hands clamped over brown paper packages. Church linens, no doubt, altar cloths and such, laundered and ironed. They see Bernice. They wave. Bernice waves back. Then she leans forward, pretending she's busy with something in the glove box. They take their time passing in front of her car. Theresa and Eloise lost their husbands and found new men to serve — the priests. Their ultimate ambition is to wash the bishop's undergarments.

When she was president of the Catholic Women's League, Bernice discovered how flawed these holy men are. Father Murphy — his new posting was a village in Quebec where he would serve a needy diocese. She hosted the going-away reception at her home. She spent her meagre household allowance on fancy ingredients and devoted hours to baking. Then she discovered, a mere month later, that he'd quit the priesthood, relocated to Lennoxville, and married a former nun from the convent in Antigonish. Apparently, their affair had been going on for years. After that, Bernice resigned from the league.

Theresa and Eloise stop by the rear door of the cathedral and put their heads together. They look back, and Bernice realizes they're talking about her. They enter. Bernice's vision telescopes into the future. She envisions Father Fraser in the pulpit, staring at her, directing his sermon about sin and hell to her. Theresa and Eloise, in their privileged seats near the altar, will follow the priest's gaze. From among the hundred congregants, their eyes will find and fix on Bernice. And because they're staring at her, the whole town will know.

Damn this town! It was definitely not Bernice's choice. Gordon felt grateful that he landed a professorship so soon after getting his doctorate, and in his home province. She loved Montreal, where they met and dated, but she agreed to keep an open mind and try Antigonish for a year. Their first baby was on the way, and she instinctively wanted to nest.

Most of the locals, including Gordon, could trace their Celtic heritage in Nova Scotia back generations. Bernice's roots were in Ontario. When his contract came up for renewal, Gordon urged her to give Antigonish one more year. Bernice was expecting the second baby when he surprised her by buying a house. After he signed on for the third year, Bernice reminded herself that marriage is about give and take. When he accepted the offer of tenure (without consulting her), she saw that it was her give and his take. He was Mr. Big Guy on Campus. She was the Little Woman in a Catholic Town where the average family had eight children. She'd do her part, but she promised herself she would never become a baby-making machine like so many of the other wives. When she finally accepted that they were staying put, she decided to make an effort to fit in by joining the Catholic Women's League.

Although it's 1975, Bernice feels that they're still in the Dark Ages. Women marched and got the vote and burned their bras but, she thinks, I'm still a prisoner. Worse than the men who are keeping me down are women like those two old crones, Theresa and Eloise.

After Gordon died, when she suggested that she might move away, the ladies of the town told her, "Oh, you can't leave now, Bernice. You're one of us."

At home, she's oppressed by another female, the caboose — her sixteen-year-old daughter, Marcia. When Bernice returned from her cross-Canada trip, Marcia proclaimed that she was perfectly capable of managing without her mother. In fact, she claimed, "I function better without you." She suggested Bernice go on another trip and stay away longer.

When Bernice was a teenager, she'd thought that there would be no plight more horrifying than becoming her mother. Is this what happens to girls — they reject their mothers, just before they become them?

Rage shoots through Bernice, like she's been pierced by a hot spear. She decides, Antigonish is not going to get my sin.

Suddenly her car is running, and she finds herself speeding out of the parking lot. Bernice brakes at the stop sign at the bottom of the hill. She's at a loss about where to go. Not home. There's a perfectly adequate church in New Glasgow. It's only thirty miles away, a nice drive for a sunny Sunday. Why not?

Act 2 – Maternal Instinct on Hold

The highway hums under her tires. This new route is so much faster than the old winding road. The asphalt at Brierly Brook is grey and fresh. It has been recently scarred with weaving black tire tracks. Some drunk teen, Bernice figures, late at night in his father's truck. She pictures Theresa and Eloise kneeling on folded towels, scrubbing the rubber tracks off the fresh pavement.

The Trans-Canada truly does unite the country. Coast to coast, from Newfoundland, across the continent to British Columbia, almost five thousand miles. Bernice lets loose a huge sigh. If only . . . if only, instead of flying, she had driven across the country. The station wagon is old but durable. A flat tire or two, even a breakdown wouldn't have been the end of the world. Then, after she'd visited Margaret Ann in Banff, she could have used the excuse that she was too intimidated by the mountains to drive through the Rockies. Or that by Alberta she was running low on money. Anything to avoid Vancouver.

At first, her trip was perfect. She flew to Montreal and the two kids there wanted to see the boarding house where she'd met their father, the bars he took her to, the restaurants where they'd eaten. Montreal was like a saucy tart — like a bolt of silk painted with gaudy colours — and Bernice still loved it.

In Toronto, Peter splurged on shows and museums, paying for everything and letting everyone, including Bernice, know how much it was costing him. Then the twins in Calgary wanted her to love Alberta beef as much as they did. Every day they ate huge steaks, starting with steak and eggs for breakfast.

After accommodating all those diverse personalities, she was looking forward to quiet time with Casey. He was not athletic; she was counting on subdued activities, like watching movies. At the last minute, Casey cancelled. When she'd written with her plan, Casey was in Edmonton, working as a short order cook. But as she made her way across the country, he had quit Edmonton and moved north for a job that paid twice as much. He claimed Fort McMurray was a redneck frontier town, too rowdy for her to visit. So she continued on to Banff, where Margaret Ann welcomed her with open arms. This daughter loved the rugged outdoors and dragged Bernice with her, hiking up mountains and rafting wild rivers. If only she'd turned back after Banff, after Margaret Ann, the last of the deserving children. Then there wouldn't have been all the business with Anger in Vancouver.

Bernice puts on her signal and turns off the highway, onto the ramp into New Glasgow. How Anger came to have that nickname is a story that got told at family gatherings, when Gordon was still alive and only when Anger wasn't around. It started one evening with Gordon complaining that Bernice wasn't fun anymore, that she was always whining about being exhausted. He said that if she was really tired, maybe it was low iron or something. Shouldn't she see a doctor? At that moment, she was washing the supper dishes. He was still at the table sipping his tea and eating the pumpkin pie she'd made from scratch (because he didn't like canned pumpkin in his pumpkin pie). The new television was babysitting the older kids. The baby in the highchair, teething, chewed on his fists and whined.

Bernice left the sink and sat before her husband. She detailed the work she'd done so far that day. Then she listed the chores that remained before she could crawl into bed beside him. "It's like this every day," she said. And on top of the daily regime, there were frequent medical emergencies — broken bones, cuts needing stitches, Casey with his recurring asthma.

Gordon interrupted to gallantly state, "That's something I can help with, emergencies." Bernice was hopeful. When Margaret Ann broke her collarbone, Gordon took her to the hospital. After that one time, he never happened to be around when disaster struck. She reminded him of his offer to help. He came up with the idea that they take turns naming the newborns. He saw from her expression that she was not placated.

"You can name the next one," he said, as if that would make her happy.

While still in hospital, Bernice announced she would name their sixth child Anastasia.

Gordon raised his hand like a traffic cop. "Dreadful name," he said. He wanted Mary, to go with the twins, Peter and Paul. She reminded her husband of their agreement. It was her turn, plain and simple. He left the room, saying, "Never! I'd prefer you name the baby after me!" When he returned the next day to take her and the baby home, they weren't talking.

Suddenly it was Sunday and the baptism was upon them. They still hadn't talked to each other. At the church, they found they were stuck with forgetful old Father Vincent. All the kids and relatives circled the baptismal font. The adults desperately needed their cup of tea. The infant was screaming her head off. The priest asked, "The name of this one?" At the same moment that Bernice proclaimed "Anastasia," her husband said, "Gordon." She repeated, "Anastasia." Gordon overlapped with his name again. Father Vincent said, "Anna Gordon?"

Anna Gordon's brothers and sisters couldn't get their little tongues around the long name. They called her Anger. Because of her temper, Bernice didn't correct them.

My precious babies, Bernice thinks. When they were little, Bernice marvelled at them from behind mountains of laundry. She glimpsed them chasing each other through the kitchen as she deboned the chicken carcass. They were endearing, but whenever she wanted to take a picture, the camera was out of film or the flashbulbs were all used up. In the end, the only time she could pause long enough to admire her children was when they were sleeping.

With the teasing and quarreling and tears, there was never a quiet moment. Sibling rivalry. After she learned that it was a normal social condition, she let them duke it out. What a cruel joke — each one born with a perfect little body. Then they launch into battle, hurting themselves and collecting souvenir scars. Margaret Ann, the eldest, didn't have a friend among her siblings because she was their dreaded commander-in-chief. The twins were always buddies. The others shifted alliances. Casey and Anger were chums. He protected his younger sister. He was gentle with her, at least in the beginning. Bernice is sure of it.

On the day Anger left home for good, she proclaimed that Bernice was a failure as a mother, cold and unloving. Anger said she'd never been hugged.

What does Anger know about love? Bernice remembers the day she carried her out of the hospital. Gordon walked ahead with her small suitcase. A car came speeding through the parking lot. How she clutched her precious bundle to her chest, this sacred parcel of new life. She would have sacrificed her own body to save her newborn. Then to be accused of not loving? Well, to hell with maternal instinct, Bernice decided. I have to be in self-preservation mode to survive this offspring of mine.

Please God, make Anger a mother. Listen God — this is my prayer: Anger gets married (poor man). Her husband leaves her (of course). Her baby is colicky, yes, crying *all the time*. And Anger, who was too good for university, has tired of waitressing. She's taking correspondence courses from home. She studies at the kitchen table in her windowless basement apartment. She's put the crib in the kitchen, where she sits at the table to study. The baby cries. I arrive, and I pick up that baby, and that baby stops crying. Anger looks up from her books. Her eyes ooze gratitude at me, her saviour. I have rescued her from insanity. And then I say, "All he needed, Anger, was a hug. Why wouldn't you hug him?"

Bernice follows the curved driveway into the parking lot of New Glasgow's Our Lady of Lourdes. She backs in so that she's facing the honest little church. It's such a contrast to the pomposity of her home parish. She's heard the jokes about Antigonish, that it's the "Little Vatican" and the "other Holy City." It will be easier to confess here in a modest, unpretentious church, right?

A vehicle arrives and parks beside her. A young man in a dark suit hurries around to open the passenger door. A woman emerges with a swaddled infant in her arms. Kids tumble from the back seat. More cars arrive: grandparents, aunts, and uncles and cousins. The priest walks out of the church. He pauses at the top of the steps. He's dressed in a long white robe and a green stole. Exploiting the theatricality of the moment, he greets his faithful parishioners with a slow, majestic wave.

Definitely a baptism. Bernice has seen more than her share of them. She realizes with sudden shock that she no longer believes in the Sacrament of Baptism. A newborn baby, tarnished with Original Sin? These edicts that she's expected to accept on faith are incomprehensible.

Bernice feels someone staring at her. Beside her car, a frozen tableau: a cluster of kids behind the father, who supports the woman's elbow. The mother holds her baby close, as if to protect the infant from the strange woman in the car. The wife asks something; her husband shrugs.

The church chimes out the hour. Each one of the reverberations repels Bernice from the family, the church, and the priest on the steps.

Truro — forty minutes down the highway. Nobody gives a hoot what she does with her Sunday.

Act 3 – Behind the Wall

This stretch of the Trans-Canada is straight but tarnished with more criss-crossed tire tracks. Bernice tut-tuts, critical of the errant teen who left these marks. Theresa and Eloise won't live long enough to scrub off all these tire tracks.

Then Bernice realizes there's a new voice inside her, an emerging personality celebrating the spirited daredevil who is the author of these tracks. She hopes it was a girl, driving her own truck, out here alone late at night laying rubber, leaving crazy figure eights on the fresh asphalt. Bernice doesn't know what to make of her new duality, battling for supremacy. She's familiar with the retiring, conservative faculty wife and knows how to play that role. But this scary wild woman who wants to break rules — where did she come from? Was she always there, waiting for her chance to break free? Bernice's mind wanders back out west, settling in Vancouver, that dreadful, wonderful night.

Anger wouldn't come to the airport. She gave Bernice detailed instructions about how to get to downtown Vancouver by public transit with many transfers. Bernice took this in stride, like any inconvenienced but uncomplaining parent. Lots of opportunity to get even later. It was agreed that they'd meet at the downtown bus terminal. Anger was late — an hour late — giving Bernice time to reflect on their correspondence. Anger had written, "Don't expect me to be your free tour guide." All her adult children were employed, except Anger. What kept her too busy to show her mother the sights?

There were five who lived together in the hippie house. Only Anger and Jerome were around. Three of the residents were hitchhiking to Tofino. Bernice was told she could sleep on the sofa in the living room. Anger hadn't thought to ask her flatmates if Bernice could stay in one of their rooms.

Of all the residents, Jerome was the only one working. He joked about his job, how he used to be a garbage collector but was now a sanitation engineer.

"The new name comes with a pay raise. I'm not goin' back to being a garbage man."

Anger didn't seem ready to accept that by 1975 the hippie era was over. She embraced the philosophy, blaming capitalism for her shitty life. Because of capitalism, she was denied what she believed was her due: a meaningful job at a high wage. While Anger made the pasta (macaroni and cheese with canned peas), she told Bernice that when she got on social assistance, it included a consultation with a social worker and that led to free sessions with a psychiatrist. The psychiatrist had given them an appointment the next morning at ten a.m.: daughter and mother. It wasn't a request, Bernice realized, as she watched her daughter sprinkle brewer's yeast on top of the macaroni.

The Church of the Immaculate Conception has a historical placard. Bernice pulls up to read it. It explains that the church's magnificent size is a testament to Truro's prosperity in the years leading up to its completion in 1871. Pulling into the parking lot, Bernice is surprised to find it full. Then she spots the hearse. She's too late to see the sombre men carrying in the casket. Everyone is already inside for the funeral. She finds it anticlimactic to sit in front of a church with the giant doors already solidly shut.

She remembers that distant funeral she attended twenty-odd years ago for Gordon's mother, who never liked her. Bernice had been grateful to have a fussy babe in arms. It meant she could stand in the back by the doors, ready to slip out. The baby — Casey — was experimenting with all the new sounds he could make. A good-looking man was also standing there, a stranger from out of town. Casey pointed a chubby finger at the man and said his new word: "Daddy." The stranger grinned at her, and Bernice grinned back. Bernice wondered if they were both thinking the same thing. She was thinking, I wish I'd had sex with this handsome stranger. Imagine making love and having that face to look at!

Casey started off as a contented baby. He grew into a happy little boy. What changed him? She remembers a

Sunday afternoon. Casey entered the kitchen and stood there. He was still short, before his growth spurt. He said "Mom" so plaintively it got her attention. He was ten or eleven, but he sounded like a tiny child.

Bernice was on the usual treadmill, darting between caring for the kids and preparing dinner. She would be serving sixteen, counting Gordon's out-of-town colleagues. If it had been just the meal, she could have managed, but there was a baby in the Jolly Jumper in the doorway; a toddler in the high chair, banging her spoon; and one of the older boys under a blanket on the chesterfield, down with the mumps. Bernice told Casey he'd have to wait. "In the meantime," she said, "you can take out the garbage. Then set the table." When Casey didn't complain, didn't whine that the other kids should be helping, she knew something was wrong.

Why did everything fall to her? The older kids knew when she needed help and made themselves scarce, like their father. What was Gordon's excuse? He had to entertain his colleagues with pre-dinner drinks in the faculty lounge.

After making the gravy, and before the pie needed to come out of the oven, she'd have to run upstairs. A wife must have her face put on and present herself in a crisply ironed dress and high heels. More and more, Bernice relied on bright red lipstick. It deflected attention away from her deficiencies and created the impression that she was in control, the breezy housewife they were all counting on.

Bernice glanced at Casey. He'd finished his chores and was waiting for her. He was not himself, one hand in and out of his pocket, the other rubbing his new crewcut. Boys don't cry. She didn't teach him that, nor did his father, but the lesson had been driven home by his friends. A boy who cries is a sissy. If only he had cried. Then she would have left the gravy and she would have gone to him. Instead she called out, "Okay, Casey, what is it?"

Did he detect the impatience in her voice? Yes. Was she scolding him for needing her? Yes.

The boy ran from the room.

No, she was not a perfect parent, but she did love her children. What Bernice expected at the psychiatrist's was that Anger would complain that Bernice was a bad mother, the accusation Anger had made the day she left home.

A degree in psychology was not necessary to read the psychiatrist. Lounging in his comfy chair, he literally rolled up his sleeves, ready to smooth feathers — or pluck them — whichever was required. Bernice already had her defence prepared, and she launched into it, strategizing that it would be to her advantage to make the first thrust.

"I'm sorry, Anger, but my hands were full. Diapers and three meals a day, laundry, baths — I'd like to see anyone raise eight kids and have time for hugs."

Anger was invited to respond, coaxed even. But her lips were pressed tightly closed. So Bernice added, "We don't need Dr. Spock to tell us that there's no such thing as a perfect parent."

The psychiatrist seemed satisfied. There, family laundry aired. He closed his file folder.

Then Anger jumped up and dropped the bomb. Her older brother, Casey, had molested her. It happened right in the family home. Many times, over several years. She accused her mother of knowing that it was happening and turning a blind eye.

Bernice felt like she was falling off a cliff. Her hands reached out to clutch something, anything to slow her fall, but she knew nothing could save her. She didn't doubt it was true because she'd seen the change in Casey. He had become cruel. Small cruelties at first. He killed Peter's baby crow. He teased the twins into a frenzy of tears. She saw these worrisome things, but she never thought he'd do the unspeakable. That critical Sunday afternoon in the kitchen — it would have been after benediction at the cathedral. Casey always assisted at benediction. He'd refused to be an altar boy after that. She'd never seen him so stubborn about anything. No explanation — but then did she ask for one? No, she did not. That was when she lost her precious son. A high metal gate shut, and he was sealed behind it. And in his anguish, he pulled his sister behind the gate with him.

Bernice fled the psychiatrist's office. She could not return to the hippie house. She urgently needed to get back home. She didn't care about the suitcase. Anger could ship it or burn it; she didn't give a shit.

It cost a small fortune to book the red-eye back to Nova Scotia. All she could think was, Anger wins. Anger has destroyed me. And I have destroyed Anger.

Bernice stares at the Truro church and wonders if a priest will be taking confession with this big funeral going on. She envisions the coffin in the aisle, and it intimidates her. She hasn't been to a funeral since Gordon's, two years ago.

Halifax, just an hour down the highway. Might as well.

Act 4 – Fallout from the Big Bang

The first crop of hay is being harvested. In the field, a tangle of teens trail behind the bailer. These would be the children of the area's farmers, harvesting at one farm and then another. This is the season when adolescent romances blossom. Girls and boys proudly show off their technique as they toss the bales up onto the truck. Would her own children have been strong enough to do this work? Probably not. Certainly not Casey with his asthma.

Casey — why did he suddenly cancel her visit when she was in Alberta? It occurs to Bernice that maybe this son didn't want to see his mother. Was saying yes to her visit and then no just another of Casey's cruelties? Or did he realize that eventually she would find out the awful truth? The wall he'd hidden behind would crumble and there he'd be, naked and guilty for everyone to see.

Driving into Halifax, Bernice's car mingles with the weekend crowd. She spies into the cars around her at each stoplight. Relaxed families, returning from the cottage or the beach, exude a bleary warmth as they drive home. Bernice recognizes that what she's feeling is nostalgia. Why in God's name does she feel nostalgic? Does she miss mothering all those kids with their endless divergent demands? No. She's relieved to be on the other side of raising a family: seven launched, only one in the nest. Does she miss being a wife? No. She and Gordon bickered constantly about who was pulling more weight. She was, of course. But because no monetary value was ascribed to a housewife's work, Gordon gave her no credit for her labour. Nobody did. It was a hard lesson to learn: that except on Mother's Day, she had no value. That's why she undertook the trip across the country. She needed to witness her life's work, her children, actualized into adulthood. Through them, she could validate herself.

Bernice read somewhere that a drastic change of altitude can affect a person's tolerance for alcohol. That day she flew into Vancouver, she descended from the Rocky Mountains — from five thousand feet — to sea level. Maybe that's why she lost control.

Anger's housemate, Jerome, reminded her of the country bumpkin on TV, on *The Beverly Hillbillies*, Jethro Bodine, a big, handsome, brainless brute. Jerome was tall and ruggedly handsome, with a playful twinkle in his eyes. As they ate the macaroni, Bernice suggested that the reason Anger chose living with others was because she grew up in a big family. But no: Anger proclaimed they were building an alternative socialist community.

"We have to, because of the mess your generation has made of everything," Anger said.

Bernice didn't respond. She was thinking, This is how we felt when we were Anger's age. We were born into a Great Depression because of a flawed economic system that people were foolish enough to buy into. Then, to recover, our politicians signed us up for a world war. Yes, our generation was disillusioned, but we were never so disrespectful as to accuse our elders.

Bernice wondered aloud, "How is your socialist community going to survive with some people taking from the system without giving back?"

Boy, did that hit a nerve.

Jerome's contribution to the communal dinner was a jug of red wine. After Bernice's comment, he filled their tumblers to the brim. He said the reason he chose to live in this house wasn't the ideology; it was the cheap rent. Then Anger said that paying rent was something her mother knew nothing about, as a woman who didn't have a job, who was taken care of her whole life by a father and then a husband. Not waiting for the rebuttal, Anger announced she was turning in. She wanted to be well rested for their important meeting with the psychiatrist in the morning. And Jerome, bless him, suggested that he and Bernice abandon the rickety kitchen chairs for the comfort of the sofa. He pulled out her chair for her.

Anger went to the bathroom and left the door open so they could hear her brushing her teeth. Jerome took little notice of her antics.

He asked Bernice, "What's the most significant change you've seen in your life?"

Bernice said that she and her husband would have had very different answers. Gordon would have said space travel, or heart transplants, or the invention of plastic. For Bernice, it was not a technological advance. She recalls vividly where she was (near the married students' residence) and how she'd felt (a sledgehammer to her heart). She had never seen it before: a young father pushing a baby carriage. The mother was nowhere in sight. Would this man also change diapers? Do laundry? Iron his own shirts? This single act gave her hope.

Gordon called feminists militant man-haters. At first, Bernice tried to make a case for the women's movement. She'd heard about private gatherings, with mirrors and women looking at themselves down there. Gordon was indignant.

"I've never heard anything so ridiculous!" he said. "As if there's anything to see!"

After that, Bernice joined him making fun of women libbers. She claimed to be content with being Mrs. Gordon

McPhail. But now, now she realizes that Gordon felt threatened, that he'd been comfortable sitting in his ivory tower and he feared he'd be toppled. With Gordon gone, Bernice realized she'd have to make up her own mind.

She asked Jerome, "If I was a young woman now, and I had children and a career, would that make me a feminist?"

Jerome laughed and topped up her glass. He said, "Drink up, buttercup."

Anger noisily closed her bedroom door.

Bernice liked that Jerome had a lightness to him, a childlike wonder. By the time they finished the jug of wine, she liked him even more. Then he darted into his room and emerged with a marijuana joint. Bernice had just one puff. Or maybe two.

Anger's bed squeaked every time she rolled over. Bernice became fixated on the bed behind the door. It took Jerome a while to figure out why Bernice had her hand clamped over her mouth. Soon they were hugging each other, laughing into each other's chests. Just when they regained control, there would be another squeak that set them off again.

The door opened and Anger stood there in a nightie.

"I'd just like to know what you're laughing at," she said.

It was good she didn't expect an answer. All she got was uproarious laughter. She slammed the door. There were no more squeaks.

Bernice doesn't remember how she and Jerome started kissing. He draped his arm over her shoulder, and his hand brushed back and forth across her nipple. At first she was scared. Then she was flattered, that this young man even saw her. She was used to not being seen. And now she was being treated as a sexual being by a man in his prime. Suddenly she was surprised to realize she was aroused.

Gordon had been her first and only. He would never do it anywhere but in bed. Every time was the same. She rarely climaxed. He did his business and thanked her for it.

This man wanted to pleasure her. Jerome found her, touched her in a way she had never been touched. Gasping for breath, she saw herself as a pomegranate burst open, the full red seeds sucked, turning her into juice. She came twice with Jerome before she'd even got his pants down. Even then, when he penetrated her, new worlds opened up. With Jerome, each muscular thrust held both power and gentleness. She met and matched him.

As they rolled off the sofa, before they hit the floor, he slipped his giant hand under her head. They landed with a loud bang. Quickly they grabbed their clothes and fled to his bedroom. In the moment she had to look around, Bernice was surprised by how orderly the room was. They picked up where they'd left off. And they kept at it until dawn.

Somewhere, way across the universe from her bodily bliss, was the realization that her daughter was sleeping. Or more likely not sleeping.

No modest church for Halifax. Bernice pulls into the vacuous parking lot and finds a spot near the back of St. Mary's Basilica. Three boys run into view. In front of Bernice's car, the smallest boy pummels the biggest with his fists. The big guy grabs him, elbow under the chin. He rubs his knuckles on the boy's head, hard. Bernice knows there's a name for that. She can't remember what it's called.

A distant voice shouts at them. The boys all look over. At the rear of the church, a priest in a black suit stands by the back door. He beckons impatiently. Altar boys, she realizes. The boys race over and file past the priest, disappearing inside the church.

Bernice has to lean forward over the dash to see the top of the basilica. These tall spires are as pompous and self-aggrandizing as priests. She's supposed to believe that God is top of the triangular hierarchy, the angels below him, the Pope, his cardinals, bishops, and then the priests. Beneath them, the people, mere mortals. Priests declare themselves the mouthpieces of God. To build these monumental churches, they bludgeoned the poor farmers and fishermen, threatened them with eternal damnation if they didn't contribute: give us your money or you'll go to hell.

Bernice knows she's still in shock because of the horrific crime that happened in her own home. She remembers the weight of her newborn baby in the hospital parking lot and her ferocious urge to protect her infant. Her heart breaks for Anger. Her heart aches for Casey too. While she cannot forgive his crime, she can forgive Casey.

Movement catches her eye. A car parks across from her. Bernice notices that the lot has filled up around her. There's a limo, too, in front of the church, decorated with Kleenex flowers. A wedding. The priest strides purposefully out of the rear door. He is now dressed in a celebratory robe and stole. He heads toward the front of the church.

Bernice's mind races: she's spent the day on the road, all to confess her sin. If she dies with this sin on her soul, she'll go to hell where she'll burn for eternity.

The priest has stopped to brush dust from the bottom of his robe.

Bernice doesn't think. Suddenly she's out of the car, striding toward the priest. She reaches him as he stands up, tall and proud of himself. He's middle-aged, and if he has any humility, it's hidden behind arrogance. He assumes she's one of his parishioners and gives a who-are-you-again tilt of his head.

"Father, is there confession? Is there a priest hearing confession now?" She's surprised at how forcefully she speaks, how loud her voice is.

"Yes, of course."

"I had sex and it was not to create a Catholic baby. It was with a man who is not my husband. It was for fun. I don't believe it was a sin."

She enjoys watching the priest's head snap back with each revelation, as if she's slapping him. Her heart is pounding as she goes on.

"Sinful sex is what's done to children. That's what should be confessed. I've decided not to confess. I'm not going to confession."

From the front of the church, someone yells out, "Father! A photograph." The priest gives her a confused look before he strides away from her.

Bernice whirls around and hurries back to her car. She glides in behind the wheel.

That word: when you grind your knuckles on the top of someone's head? It's called a noogie. Giving a noogie.

Gazing around the Halifax parking lot from the security of her car, she feels like she's in her dank basement, expects to see cans of beans. She is suffering her own personal radiation sickness. Her struggle is to forgive herself. She can do it. She can do anything. She can leave Antigonish, leave the house to the Caboose's exceptional management. She can get a job. Before she married, she was a sales clerk. She could do all sorts of things. She should definitely get a lover, now that she knows what all the fuss is about.

A horn blares. A souped-up truck idles in front of Bernice's car. A man with a ducktail haircut mouths the words, "You leaving?" He's menacing. Not the type of man to push a baby carriage. She decides, as she drives away, to trade in her station wagon for a truck. She'll find a stretch of new highway. Laying rubber on fresh asphalt is just the therapy she needs.

GREEN PANIC

I'm that hungry, I'm just going to shovel the food in with this knife, the one I use to split kindling. I have smoked salmon from up the coast, chanterelle mushrooms I picked myself, and mussels from the shore in front of my cabin. I pluck them, plump and juicy, right from the shell and dip them in garlic butter.

I've been up since seven and had a great swim around Mussel Island, which is about two kilometres at low tide. Swimming, I peered down at minnows and crabs and mackerel scurrying away from my great looming shadow, and I marvelled again at the miracle of mask and snorkel. On this morning's swim, I felt an instant kinship with Kipping because she'd said her trip to Cape Breton was "perfect" since she got to swim every day. I will, too, every day I'm here, because swimming in the unforgiving North Atlantic is life itself, though once this ocean almost killed me.

A year ago, the rip tide at Dunvegan swept me out too far. I thought of all my last words spoken. I wished my sister and I hadn't fought, because we love each other. While I swam through green panic on the inside and choppy surf on the outside, I imagined the coroner's half smile when he would discover my clip-on earrings shoved between clammy breasts and bathing suit. In that moment, did I feel that my friend the ocean would betray me? No. I felt rather that I would be betraying the ocean if I succumbed and made a killer of it.

How tenuous that sliding sand under tired, grasping toes when finally shore was won. The card-playing friends up at the wet campsite didn't know about my near death, and they finished their Tarabish championship in cheerful ignorance. I never did tell them that I'd almost stolen their lazy long weekend to replace it with a tragedy they'd never forget.

It was in the cards, after all. Vernon the Fortune Teller had seen my near death months before when packs of spring ice still hid the beach. He foretold that there would be no evidence, not a scar on my perfect flesh. Only after I'd made it back to the beach did I remember his prophecy. As I lay on the former mountains, ground now into sand by the same waves that had almost transformed me into another state of being, I realized that I was unmarked.

This year, on this morning's swim, eight feet below me, oysters clung to the rocks and a moon snail spread out big as a platter on the sand. Recalling this, I forget the knife, still in my mouth — and it slides sideways and cuts my lip.

If your only utensil is a knife, don't forget it's in your mouth. It may be a perfect day, but you don't need a scar to remember it.

KIDS ON THE PATH

When the three kids turn off Church Street, they are leaving civilization and entering the wild. To get to the river, they have to trespass, sneaking between a big white house and a weathered barn. They follow a narrow path, walking one behind the other. As they pass the smelly barn, Kathleen pictures the horse, Stormy, shitting in there all winter. Back of the barn is a fresh pile of manure. The stink is coming from there.

Micky, Kathleen's older brother, is in the lead.

"Phew," he says.

Following him is Jimmy, her youngest brother.

"Double p-hew," Jimmy says.

Micky whirls around and crouches down to be at Jimmy's eye level. "Quit saying what I say! Why don't you just go home!"

Kathleen sees the little guy press his lips together, and she knows it's to keep from crying.

"I don't know where it is," Jimmy says. Although it's only two blocks away, the house is not in sight.

Micky turns and continues on. Kathleen rumples the little boy's hair. With a gentle shove, she sends him off after his big brother. She wishes Micky would stop picking on Jimmy.

Secretly, Kathleen likes the smell of manure. Every spring, Mr. MacGillivray shovels out the barn and the stench drifts through the neighbourhood. Manure stinks. The fish plant on the other side of town stinks. Bad smells exist and they have a right to exist and we should accept them. If only she'd made that point to her mother this morning. Instead, Kathleen took the tube of deodorant and nodded when her mother insisted she apply it every day.

Old Mr. MacGillivray saddles up Stormy every summer and rides him in parades. To exercise the horse, he lets the kids ride — but only the boys. It's as if Mr. MacGillivray doesn't even see her. When she went home and complained, her mother said girls shouldn't ride horses. Kathleen asked, "What are we supposed to ride?" but there was no answer.

At the library, Kathleen asked why all the adventure stories were about boys. Boys with horses and dogs and on sailboats and on rafts. The librarian, Miss Henry, stacked her up with books about Marie Curie and Helen Keller and Amelia Earhart. Kathleen wants to be like Annie Oakley, shooting coins tossed in the air. Back in the 1800s, women could do anything they set their minds to. What can a girl do these days? She's supposed to get excited about waving Canada's new flag at the centennial celebration — whoopee shit. If only she lived in California or anywhere in the States, instead of this dull country. If she was born a hundred years ago, instead of 1955, she wouldn't have to wear deodorant.

Being a girl just keeps getting worse. At first, breasts started growing on her chest and they hurt. Her mother said that

Kathleen was becoming a woman (as if that was a good thing) and promised that eventually her breasts would stop being so tender. Then Kathleen started her stupid period. She didn't know what was going on — she thought she was bleeding to death and stopped riding her bicycle. Cramps hurt more than budding breasts. Nobody told her growing up would hurt this much.

This summer when Mr. MacGillivray saddles up Stormy, she'll jump up on the horse and ride away so fast they can't catch her!

Kathleen adjusts the coil of rope on her shoulder. Looking over Jimmy's head at Micky's back, she wishes she was in the lead. One thing for sure — when she grows up she won't be a follower. She'll be the boss. She thought she'd work in a library until Miss Henry mentioned that they (her bosses?) won't let her have books like *Catcher in the Rye* (whatever that is) and *Fanny Hill*. Kathleen already read *Fanny Hill* — she found it hidden under her brother Ben's mattress. She only had two days to read it while he was away at a basketball game. It made her decide not to get married, since having sex is so painful.

Jimmy is chattering. The little guy is rhyming something. He's going through the names of the kids in the family, youngest to oldest.

"Jimmy, Kathleen, Micky, Bernice, Ben. Begin again. Jimmy . . ."

He says a name with each step. Except her name. Kathleen gets three steps because he's divided it into syllables: Kath-O-Leen.

"Jimmy, Kath-O-Leen, Micky, Bernice, Ben. Begin again."

Secretly she's flattered that his litany gives her three steps. Sometimes he calls her Katie. Sure, Jimmy can be annoying as heck, but he's a pretty special kid.

They get to the end of the field and are at the edge of the woods. Micky tells them they have to hide in the trees and wait and watch.

"Gotta make sure we're not being followed."

Nobody will be following, Kathleen thinks. Who cares what they get up to as long as they're home for supper. But she slips in behind him and tucks Jimmy beside her. From the cover of trees, they peer out.

The world Micky lives in is full of murderers. Kathleen knows because she regularly checks what book is beside his bed, and he's always reading a murder mystery. Kathleen tried one, but the story felt too made up. Stacked beside her bed, she has the maximum allowable library books. It's not just her bedroom — she has to share with her sister, Bernice, who has magazines like *Seventeen* and *Teen-Agers Hairdos*. They're mostly makeup tricks and pickup tips. "Twenty ways to make him fall for you." If Bernice read *Fanny Hill,* she wouldn't be so keen on boys.

Bernice flipped through Kathleen's copy of *Old Yeller* and found out it's about a boy and his dog, so she called her a tomboy. Kathleen pretended to be hurt, but she was flattered. Boy is better than girl.

As they hide, Micky has been watching Kathleen bite dead skin off her chapped bottom lip.

"Don't eat that!" Micky whispers hoarsely.

Kathleen doesn't know what he's talking about.

"That skin. I saw you bite off skin from your lip and it's in your mouth," he says.

"So?" She deliberately chews.

"You're a cannibal."

Jimmy springs to his sister's defence. "A people isn't a cannonball."

"Cannibal, Jimmy," Micky corrects him.

"That's what I said. She can't be a cannonball."

"Butt out," says Micky.

"You cursed."

"I did not!"

"You said *butt*. That's a dirty word. I'm telling."

"Listen, you little twerp." Micky grabs Jimmy's shirt and yanks him close. "Keep your mouth shut or go home."

Micky clips Jimmy's head. Kathleen sees fear in Jimmy's face.

"Don't hit him." Kathleen grabs Jimmy's small hand. She feels the wart on the palm of Jimmy's hand, and she wants to let go but she doesn't. They push past Micky, and simple as that, they're in the lead.

Over her shoulder, she tells Micky, "A cannibal eats other people. I eat myself."

"Not a cannonball!" Jimmy shouts back.

The loyal little guy holding her hand has been spanked, their mother spanks them all. Kathleen asked around and found out that her friends' parents spank their kids. Not all fathers use the belt. Their father does, but so far only on the boys. At school, they use the strap. Some teachers, like Miss McLeod, find someone to strap every day. Kathleen wonders what hurts more — the strap or her father's belt on a naked bum.

Kathleen was eight when she was strapped for the first time. She and Bonnie spelled three of the four oceans wrong. Miss McLeod called them up to the front of the class and strapped Kathleen first. The shock of the pain took her breath away. It hurt more than anything she'd ever felt. She was strapped five times on each hand. The whole agonizing time she felt Bonnie's eyes on her. Since Bonnie got the strap every day and never cried, Kathleen forced herself not to.

When she came home from school that day, Kathleen wanted to tell her mother; she wanted to cry and let the hurt out. But her mother would have sided with the teacher so she cried into her pillow.

Afterwards, Kathleen and Bonnie were friends for a while. They went to each other's houses to play. Now that she thinks about it, Bonnie is the only Black kid in the class. Does that have something to do with her daily strappings? Adults say, "Spare the rod, spoil the child." It's not like Bonnie is spoiled.

Jimmy has been spanked but he's never been strapped, never had the belt. In a way, he's not ruined. Micky has been strapped and belted and he's mean. Does everybody start off good? Does being beaten make good people turn bad? Are wars started by people who have been mistreated? Kathleen knows she'll need a lot of years to learn the answers to these big questions. In the meantime, she hopes she can protect Jimmy.

The new leaves on the willow and birch branches are tiny and vividly green. After the long grey winter, Kathleen cannot bear the thought of killing even one precious leaf. Where the path is narrow, she twists her shoulders to avoid touching the branches. Wherever the path dips, there's a puddle of spring runoff. She leads Jimmy around them, but the grassy borders are soggy. Her old sneakers leak, and cold water seeps in and chills her feet.

Jimmy pulls his hand free. He runs ahead to a perfect puddle. Before Kathleen can stop him, he leaps into the deep middle of it, pounding his boots up and down like a jack-in-the-box. Water sprays all the way to his waist, then as high as his head.

"Jimmy! No!" Kathleen yells.

When he stops, he's surprised that Kathleen and Micky are both glaring at him. He reaches for the top of his head and discovers a clot of mud. Looking down, he sees his whole body is splattered. Kathleen watches his expression fall as he realizes why he's in trouble.

Micky slaps a tree. "I told you not to let him come!"

"No, you didn't," says Kathleen.

"I'm not taking the blame for this." He stomps into the puddle and clips Jimmy's head, not hard, then marches him forward. Suddenly Micky stops, staring at his sneakers. They're white — were white — and are now wet and muddy. He'd taken such care walking around the puddles.

For Micky's birthday last week, a shoebox appeared on the table before him. He took out the Converse sneakers, examined the spotless treads, and even leaned down to sniff them.

"Let me smell them too," Jimmy had said.

Kathleen saw the look on Micky's face when he realized nobody had worn them before. Until now, it had always been hand-me-downs from his older brother. Micky actually hugged his dad. The old fart suddenly had to go out for a smoke.

It made Kathleen happy for Micky, but Bernice leaned in and whispered, "Just goes to show, if you make them miserable enough, they'll give you what you want."

Micky whispered back, "What I really want is high tops, but these'll get the attention of the girls."

Micky's always telling Kathleen that he's going to be rich. He's saving to buy a Mustang convertible, red of course. At sixteen, he'll get his licence, and by seventeen, he hopes to have enough for a down payment on the car. Kathleen believes he just might do it. She found his metal box stashed in the crawl space behind his bed, and already he's got sixty-two dollars in there. Micky's secret ambition is that before he's twenty, he'll be making more money than his father. He wants to rub that in the old man's face.

Jimmy runs off ahead and Micky follows, growling and stomping his wet feet. Their father better not see that Micky's sneakers are dirty — he'd get the belt for that.

Where the path hits the river, it splits to left and right. Jimmy and Micky have stopped and Kathleen joins them, looking at the bubbling river. At this time of year, Brierly Brook, gorged with spring runoff, is more river than brook. There are exciting swirling eddies and dark frothy pools. They look for the stepping stones they laid last summer when the water was low. Kathleen spots them a foot below the surface and points them out. The water flows smoothly over the stones, then curls up like the flip in Annette Funicello's hair.

The boys move on, but Kathleen stays. The path to the left leads to her tree, the willow with the long branch, and she can't leave without getting a look at it. She peers past the overhanging alders so she can see her magnificent willow. The long, fat branch that stretches out over the flowing water is wide enough for her to lie on. It's her sacred, private place where nothing can touch her. The tree even saved her from her father.

Every day, her father comes home, complains about his boss at the fish plant, eats, beats the boys, and goes to bed. Kathleen was sick of hearing him talk about how rich he'd be if he didn't have kids. Now that she knew how kids are made, she heard herself say, "You have something to do with us being here." When she saw his hands go to his belt, she lit out of the house. Kathleen was more terrified than she'd ever been in her life. She heard her father's feet thunder down the back steps behind her. She sprinted, the way they taught her at track and field. His strained panting became less audible as they approached the river. At the willow tree, her feet flew up the wooden slats she'd hammered on the trunk. She shimmied out on the branch until she was hidden by leaves. Her father thrashed around in the bushes below, calling and calling for her. On her high branch, she discovered a new power. She didn't need to answer; she could avoid getting beaten. Through the leafy branches, she watched him leave. Her father, she decided, was the most boring, useless father in the world.

She waited until everyone had gone to bed, then snuck in through a basement window and tiptoed up the basement stairs. Creeping through the kitchen, she saw a body slumped in a chair, head on the table, asleep. Her father looked small, defenceless. She saw that he was just a man, caught with a family he had to support and a job he deplored. Kathleen went closer to him, was ready to wake him up when she saw, in the dim light, something round on the table. It was his belt, coiled like a snake and ready to strike.

That night, she made a bed on the basement floor with damp towels from the laundry basket. Kathleen made an oath that she would never be the outlet for his anger. She has kept her distance from the man who takes revenge on his children.

Kathleen takes the path to the left, hurrying to catch up with her brothers. The path follows the river, weaving in and out of trees along the bank. As she comes closer to the secret hideaway, Kathleen has a sick feeling in her stomach. Her friends call it the Garden of Eden, but Kathleen can't help hearing another name roaring in her head: the Garden of Evil.

Inside a thick cluster of alders is a clearing, obscured by interwoven branches. If you didn't know it was there, you would just walk past. You have to get down on all fours and crawl in, pushing the branches aside. There's enough space in the clearing for a group of kids to get up to no good, and a few weeks ago they did.

There are four in her gang — Kathleen and the three Ms: Margaret, Marion, and Mary. They've been best friends since grade four. Kathleen likes being the leader because in the future, when she's a boss, she'll need to get people to obey her. It's her job to come up with ideas and get everyone to execute them.

The last class of the day was religion, and Miss McLeod wrote on the blackboard, "The Fall from Grace." In the Garden of Eden, Adam was lonely so God created a woman from his rib. The serpent tempted the naked couple, Eve took the forbidden apple, made Adam eat it, and suddenly they're ashamed. Then they're banished into the Valley of Tears . . . Blah, blah, blah. Kathleen had heard this story since she was little. What's the point?

Miss McLeod's point was that now that they were women (the girls rolled their eyes), they would encounter snakes who would tempt them. Modesty of thought and action was the message. Women were temptresses capable of causing the downfall of mankind. Breasts were to be hidden. Everything below the waist was dark, forbidden territory.

Miss McLeod stared them down until they all felt ashamed of their bodies and guilty of the crime of being a woman. When she released them from class, they felt like they could destroy all humankind if they weren't careful.

In the hallway, Kathleen saw the crestfallen faces of the three Ms and knew they needed rescuing. She pointed to their frumpy, middle-aged teacher disappearing into the staff room and whispered that Miss McLeod was a virgin. She knew nothing about women's bodies or men's bodies or sex. It was up to them to continue their research, in *Playboy* and *Fanny Hill* and to share the snippets they gleaned in their remote corner of the schoolyard.

Marion revealed that she babysat for a non-Catholic couple and discovered *Guide for Newlyweds* hidden in the cabinet near their bed. It even had illustrations! If they wanted, Marion could recommend them for babysitting; they would have to pay her what they earned. While Margaret and Mary clamoured for jobs, Kathleen tried to figure out what to do next. These days, the three Ms always wanted to go to the pool hall to bum a cigarette and watch the boys shoot pool. Kathleen hated her gang's annoying flirtation with boys. She feared they were pulling away from her into different orbits. She needed to invent an exciting distraction.

All of a sudden, Lizzie MacIsaac, the new girl, was standing in front of her. Everyone ignored Lizzie so what was she doing talking to Kathleen uninvited. Kathleen stared at Lizzie's face with her buck teeth and glasses and pimples. Even after blinking several times, Kathleen saw Lizzie was still there, staring at her through her ugly cat-eye glasses. She'd asked a question.

"What?" Kathleen asked.

Lizzie took a breath and repeated. "To balance the Christian creation story, we should be taught Einstein's theory of relativity and Darwin's theory of natural selection. The class is called religion, so it shouldn't only be Catholicism, right?"

Despite Kathleen's distain for the messenger, Kathleen got the message: it was possible to question what was taught in school. But it was not up to Lizzie to tell her or her gang what to do. She found herself becoming angry. She let Lizzie chat on while she schemed. Then Kathleen convinced the three Ms to give up the pool hall and follow her to Brierly Brook. They kept giving Kathleen questioning glances. Why had she invited an outsider along?

Lizzie was so grateful she glowed like a firefly. She told Marion she liked her pink lipstick, and she complimented Margaret on her blue eyeshadow. When she said to Mary, "I like your pedal pushers," and found out she'd sewed them herself, they got talking about Simplicity Patterns.

They arrived at their secret hideaway, crawled on hands and knees into the small clearing, and stood in an awkward circle. Kathleen announced the new name for their hideaway — the Garden of Eden. Like Adam and Eve, they would all get naked and re-enact the Fall from Grace. Instantly, the three Ms got it: they understood why the new girl was there. They did Kathleen's work for her, talking Lizzie into stripping first.

Then Kathleen piped up. "Out of respect for Lizzie's modesty, we should wait outside."

When Lizzie reported, in a high, thin voice, that her clothes were off, Kathleen told her to hand them out. Lizzie didn't say or do anything.

Kathleen fixed her eyes on Mary and asked, "Who wants to go next?"

"Me, please," Mary said. "Let me go next!"

"Okay, Mary, you can go in as soon as Lizzie hands out her clothes."

There was still no response from inside. Kathleen thrust her arms through the brambles into the clearing.

"Oh hurry up, Lizzie! I want to go in," Mary said with enough conviction that Kathleen's hands emerged with a folded stack of clothes sitting on new leather shoes.

The gang ran off with the clothes down the bank to the river. They giggled at the training bra and the old-fashioned modest bloomers and threw the clothes in, one item at a time. The current was swift and carried them off.

They heard Lizzie call out, "Hey! You guys?"

When she kept calling, the pitch getting higher and higher, the fun was over. Kathleen and the three Ms ran to the playground. They hung out for a while on the monkey bars, but it wasn't fun so they went home.

Ahead, Kathleen hears Micky calling for her. She hurries to where the path slopes down the bank, ending on a wide, gravely beach. Micky calls again, impatient. She joins him by the neatly stacked eight-foot long treated timbers. They discovered them a while back and at first couldn't figure how they ended up abandoned here. Then they remembered the train station downriver and realized these were railway crossties. Kathleen and Micky argued back and forth about whether they belonged to anyone, but they kept coming back to how perfect they were for a raft. After that, they didn't care if the railway company owned them or not.

Kathleen had told Micky they had to research how to build a raft. At the library, she pulled out *Robinson Crusoe* and *Tom Sawyer*, books with drawings and diagrams. Micky reminded her, "Just because you're good with books doesn't mean you're smarter than me."

Kathleen stacked the books on a table and pulled up a chair. Micky wouldn't sit down, and she realized it was because he'd got the belt. Did the librarian figure it out too? When Kathleen was checking out, Miss Henry included an extra book and said pointedly, "There are lessons here for everyone." At first, Kathleen couldn't figure out why she should read it. Miss Henry was weird sometimes. Maybe it was true what they said, that she was a lesbian. The life of Mahatma Gandhi way over there in India was remote and unimaginable.

The ties are heavy so they carry them individually to the river. Jimmy is no help — he keeps getting underfoot so they send him away. It takes all their strength to haul the first one to the water's edge. With the second one, they discover it's easier to roll it. After the third, they decide they have enough to get started. Placing two timbers beside each other, they push them half in the water and half out. Kathleen and Micky take off their sneakers and wade into the river. They fight the cold and the current as they lash the far ends together and then the middle. They are using the last of the rope on the end that is on dry shore when Jimmy calls out, "I gotta go to the bathroom."

"There's no bathroom — use the great outdoors," Kathleen says.

Jimmy, hands on hips, doesn't budge.

Micky taunts, "Don't you know how to pee outdoors?"

"Nobody never showed me."

"Sissy."

Jimmy sticks his arms straight down, his fists curled up tight. Kathleen wonders if other families are like this, picking on each other. Are the older siblings always mean to the younger ones? But she's older than Jimmy and she doesn't pick on the little guy. Kathleen tosses the ends of the rope to Micky so he can finish the tying. Carefully she picks where she puts her bare feet. Jimmy happily takes her hand and lets himself be led to a bush. He pushes her away so he can take care of business himself.

After the Fall from Grace, Lizzie didn't come to school for a week. When she reappeared, she kept completely to herself. She wouldn't look at the gang. That made it easier for them to pretend that nothing serious had happened. But then Kathleen found herself telling Miss McLeod that religion class should be renamed Catholic class unless it taught all religions. Miss McLeod determined that Kathleen was having a crisis of faith and should have a talk with a priest. When Kathleen didn't back down, the teacher conceded, "I'd have to get permission from the school board to teach other beliefs."

Miss McLeod felt the need to deter Kathleen from challenging the curriculum ever again. She assigned her a week of cleaning the chalk brushes. Kathleen didn't see it as punishment. She was fighting the good fight for everyone — but especially for Lizzie. She watched for the right moment to tell her that she'd acted on her suggestion. As the chalk dust flew out of the brushes, Kathleen reflected on this new revelation: that a teacher needed board approval. She had considered becoming a principal or a teacher. So much for that career. She now envisioned a crowd of women and men sitting in a circle, knitting the net they drop over the school to keep new ideas out.

When you're looking at two timbers lashed together, it takes imagination to see a raft, but that's what Kathleen and Micky see.

"This raft needs a test run," Micky says, "with someone on it."

Kathleen shakes her head. "The river's too high now. We should tie it up and come back when the river's not as fast."

"Tie it up with what? Do you see any rope?"

"Besides we can't steer without a pole."

They hear Jimmy returning before they see him, fumbling his way through a nursery rhyme. "See how they run. They all run after the farmer's wife, who cuts up the butcher's wife . . ." Jimmy stops, puzzled. He knows he's muddled the words. He's wearing something on his head that looks like big white mouse ears.

"Jimmy, what's that?" Kathleen asks. It looks vaguely familiar.

"Mine! I found it," Jimmy says. He keeps nodding his head, enjoying the way the ear-cups bob up and down. Kathleen's heart speeds up as she realizes it's a bra — Lizzie's bra — streaked with river silt.

"Give it to me," Kathleen says, approaching.

"It's mine," he shouts. He dances away from her.

In her bare feet it's hard to catch him, but Kathleen does and yanks the thing off his head. She twists away and shoves it deep into her pocket. She feels a twinge of regret for the poor kid. Jimmy's fly is down.

"Hey Jimmy-boy, I've got a treat for you!" Micky sings out as he strides over. Kathleen recognizes the walk — he has the same swagger as their father.

Being the youngest has given Jimmy a strong instinct for self-preservation.

"What?"

"Guess who gets the first ride on the raft?"

"Not me," Jimmy says, making a run for it. Even barefoot, Micky runs faster and catches up with him. He escorts the boy, gently but with a firm grip, toward the raft.

Jimmy twists around so he can see Kathleen. "Make him stop!"

Kathleen feels disconnected, like she's an actor in someone else's play. With her gang she's in control, but this is Micky's idea. At the raft, Micky lifts the boy and carries him out into the water. He plunks him down in the middle of the raft.

"Hold on." Micky slams Jimmy's hand on the centre rope.

Kathleen realizes this shouldn't be happening. "Stop, Micky!" she shouts. She splashes into the river and grabs Micky's arm.

He shoves her away. He rocks the raft to free it.

Kathleen shouts, "No!" She pushes down on the raft, trying to keep it from moving.

"Your fault. You should have got on."

Mickey gives a mighty push that frees the raft. Caught instantly by the current, it swings away from the shore. Micky stands transfixed, watching the raft whirling around and away.

"Damn kid is too light," he says.

"I can't swim," Jimmy squeals.

Kathleen runs along the shore following the raft, shouting "Jimmy!"

Micky stumbles along behind her. The beach stones are sharp under their feet. The boy waves both arms in the air, screaming for help.

"Jimmy! Hold on to the rope!" Kathleen yells.

The beach ends and Kathleen and Micky are stopped by a thick cluster of brush. The raft is about to go around the bend, where it will be out of sight.

"I'm scared!" Jimmy screams, loud enough to be heard across the noisy water.

Beside her, Kathleen hears Micky's heavy panting. She knows what has to be done. When she glances at Micky, she knows he won't go out there after Jimmy. It has to be her. She wades into the turbulent water. The cold takes her breath away. She lets the current carry her. Just before being swept around the bend, she glances back and sees Micky running the other way down the shore. Where's he going? Back to get his precious sneakers!

The river does most of the work for her. She's moving fast, but she's being swept into the middle of the river. The raft is closer to shore. One end bangs into a rock outcropping that spins it around. Jimmy is holding on with one hand, and the other is in the air. He looks like he's riding a bronco in a rodeo. Kathleen paddles and kicks, trying to get closer to the raft. Ahead she sees a willow extending from the bank, its branches hanging in the river. The raft is heading straight for it.

"Jimmy, look ahead! Duck."

Kathleen sees the raft get caught in the willow's branches. The current carries the back end of the raft around, anchoring it against the shore.

Jimmy, still clinging to the rope, looks around frantically. He sees Kathleen.

"Help me!"

Kathleen kicks as hard as she can. She's getting closer, but the current is stronger than she is. She overshoots the raft. As she's swept past, she sees Jimmy's anguished face. He mouths something she can't hear.

With all her strength, Kathleen paddles toward shore. Yard by yard, she's winning the fight. An enormous effort brings her almost within reach of the bank. She stretches her hand toward a root sticking out of the bank but can't quite reach it before the current carries her farther away. Thinking surely she can touch bottom, Kathleen drops her legs. But her toes touch nothing. Water splashes into her mouth and nostrils. She can't get a good breath. Panic surges up from her feet, clutches her whole body. The stark truth is that she could drown. To lose her life this close to shore would be cruel.

Jimmy's voice: "Kathleen!"

A stark truth hits her like a lightning bolt. If she drowns, her little brother will likely die too. The sickening fear transforms into fierce energy. She pulls her legs up from the bottom. Kicking and paddling, she fights her way to the bank. Her knees bang against something. She draws her feet up until they find a slippery mud ledge. Her fingers clutch the bank. Propelling herself up onto the shore, she marvels at her own strength.

Kathleen bushwhacks along the shore back toward the raft. Jimmy is still there, his face wet with tears and snot. He's holding the rope with both hands. She crawls out on the raft until her extended hand can reach his.

"Take my hand. It's okay, Jimmy. Let go."

He shakes his head, too scared to release his grip on the rope. Kathleen crawls out farther, sliding her hands along the rough timbers. She ignores the sting of splinters. When she gets to Jimmy, she pries his fingers loose. The boy clutches her like a mother koala bear, arms and legs wrapped around her as she crawls backwards to the bank.

As soon as they're safely, solidly on shore, Kathleen hugs Jimmy's soggy little body. She squeezes him, remembers holding him when he was newborn. That was when she started loving him. Jimmy hugs her back.

Micky's voice calling their names grows louder. Kathleen calls back. Jimmy, still scared, hides behind her.

Micky suddenly bursts through the brush. Kathleen sees that he's wearing his sneakers and carrying hers. His wild eyes take in Kathleen, then dart to the raft, and he sees it is empty. He rushes to the bank, frantically scanning the swirling river. He calls and calls for the boy.

Jimmy slides out of his hiding place behind Kathleen to stand beside her, watching their older brother. Micky darts away along the bank, still yelling. Kathleen looks down at Jimmy and he looks up at her. Neither of them say anything.

From the brush, the crashing of Micky returning.

"We gotta get help," he yells. "Kathleen?"

He emerges and sees them standing beside each other. The shock of seeing Jimmy stops Micky in his tracks but only for a moment. He races over, falls to his knees, and hugs the boy. His shoulders shake as he sobs, out-of-control crying. Jimmy, his arms pinioned to his sides, looks up at Kathleen.

"I want Mommy," he says.

Micky pulls himself back. As he shakes his head, tears stream across his face. He says, "Listen, nobody can ever know about this."

Kathleen imagines them standing in the kitchen, dirty and wet, facing her parents. Her mother inhaling sharply, her hand going up to cover her mouth. Her father's hands going to his belt.

Kathleen hears herself say, "Micky's right. No telling."

The kid's head drops to his chest.

"They'll know anyway," he says, pointing at Micky's sneakers. "Look."

No longer white or new, there's a tear in the toe of one of them and they're permanently stained. The sneakers are ruined.

Kathleen tells Micky, "Here's what you have to do. Hide those. Buy a new pair with the money in your box."

Micky turns on her. "What money?"

"In the metal box. Sixty-two dollars."

When she sees the surprise on Micky's face, she adds, "Everybody knows."

At first, Kathleen found that Mahatma Gandhi was too simple. He stated the obvious, like, "See the good in people and help them." But Kathleen discovered that she'd memorized another quote: "The weak can never forgive. Forgiveness is the attribute of the strong." She was strong so she should help others stay strong or to get their strength back. She thought of Jimmy and she thought of Micky. But if she really was strong, she had to forgive herself.

At recess, Kathleen is pounding chalk out of the brushes when she spots Lizzie sitting by herself. Underneath her is the science textbook, to keep her skirt from getting dirty. There has not been a word out of Lizzie since she returned to school, not in class or to any of her classmates. It will be up to Kathleen to initiate discussion. Abandoning the brushes, she goes to her.

Kathleen tries asking her what she's reading. No answer. She explains why she has to clean brushes, punishment from the teacher for telling her to change religion class. Lizzie stands up. She looks around to make sure there's nobody close enough to hear.

"My mother wanted to tell your parents. I wouldn't let her. Everyone would know."

It feels to Kathleen that an apology will not be enough to make reparation, but she tries anyway.

Lizzie stares at her and Kathleen recognizes that she's looking at someone far more intelligent than she is.

Lizzie says, "B-I-T-C-H," and walks away.

Kathleen doesn't have a comeback. She was a bitch when she did that awful thing. She decides that this evening, when her father comes home, she will do something to get him so angry, he'll use his belt on her naked backside.

MOTHER'S DAY

Margaret sits in an ancient rocking chair on her deck. God is in his heaven, and all is right with the world. She can't stop herself from grinning. Who cares if the old woman is grinning? Nobody can see her.

The table beside her holds a gin and tonic. On a cold day, it would be a hot rum toddy.

Today is a glorious spring day with a sun that is warm enough to bead the glass. Also on the table is a calendar with "In" and "Out" marked beside names like Bryden and John Angus and Buddy. The local weekly paper, the *Chronicle*, is open to the police report.

She's on the highest deck in town, built off the second floor of her two-storey house. The only way out to the deck is through her bedroom. Nobody gets to come here, not her friends and certainly not her overly protective adult kids. They would want to raise the railing another few feet and put a harness on her.

Beside her house is the court house adjoined by the small jail, and behind that is a fenced-in exercise yard. From her vantage point, she can see over the eight-foot fence topped with barbed wire. Every day, between three and four p.m. in every kind of weather, the prisoners are turned out.

It's almost three, and Margaret rocks in happy anticipation. She inherited the rocking chair from her mother, a nursing chair the perfect height for a mother's arms to cradle a baby's head. With her first infant, John Charles, Margaret had moved the chair to the window to alleviate the tedium of the daily feedings. One day as he suckled greedily, Margaret's glazed eyes suddenly found the prisoners being released into the yard. Who were these men? What crimes had they committed? Why had she never paid attention before? From then on, she nursed the baby, whichever baby, in the chair by the window. When the prisoners took their exercise, she'd be there to watch. She'd even wake a sleeping infant to feed it during the exercise hour. What mother would disturb a baby's sleep in those early months of life? Was she that bored, that lonely? Apparently yes. Gazing down on the prisoners, she'd felt comradeship. The endless demands from pre-verbal humans were her ball and chain. Her big house was her prison.

Poor Walter. In his world, the office at the town hall, he had control. In marriage, he was often ambushed by Margaret's obsessions. She told him she needed a deck, not on the front but on the back of the house, not on the ground level but on the second floor. She claimed it was to watch the children in the yard. From the back door, she couldn't see what they were up to, but from a high deck, she could do the mending and watch that the children didn't kill each other. They were up to dangerous games now. Hadn't Randall tied little Grace to the tree at the far end of the yard when they played Cowboys and Indians? Wasn't it hours before Margaret found the poor girl? Walter did the household accounts. When he recited the list of their expenses, he said that a deck did not appear among them. He picked up his briefcase and went to work.

Margaret packed a small suitcase. She planned to take the train to her mother's, but she had no money. Walter doled out cash as it was needed, and only the amount she needed. Groceries were purchased on credit: an account in the name of Mr. Walter MacSween. Also, she couldn't just walk out because the three youngest weren't old enough for school yet. She wouldn't let a disagreement between parents make the children suffer. She waited on the sofa, hands folded. The older kids arrived home for lunch. They sensed something was strange, so they gathered the little ones and all sat quietly at the kitchen table, waiting to be fed. When Walter came home for lunch, Margaret went to the door, put on her coat, and picked up her suitcase. She asked for money for the train. She watched his familiar face scrunch up with confusion. Then she saw hurt, replaced by fear. In all their years of marriage, through all the insecurities and the illnesses and even the two miscarriages, she had never seen him this vulnerable. He took the suitcase from her hand and led her up the stairs. In their bedroom, she spread her arms wide to describe where the wall would be cut open for the door to the new deck.

The jailor is always a Gillis. In the early years, it was Dean Gillis, with his son sometimes filling in. Dean is gone and now it's the son. Down below, she sees the door swing open. Young Gillis steps outside. One by one, the men pass out of the jailhouse and into the yard. The men, her men: Bryden and John Angus and Buddy. There's Coleman, back for another stint. Their sentences are "two years less a day," in reality just a few weeks or a couple of months before they are paroled. There's a new one. He must be a drunk and disorderly taken in last night. If he's here this late in the day, he must have taken a swing at a cop. Margaret bends over the railing. Could it be Kevin, from down the street? His father's a doctor. What an embarrassment: this disgraced son will tarnish their brass door knocker.

She's never worried about being seen. Perhaps political prisoners raise their heads, but her men, they come and go, and they never look up. Except once.

The doorbell rings. Drat! Who would dare come at this time of day? She is unavailable from three to four each day; her family and her friends have all been warned. This visitor is not someone close to her.

Margaret grips the rail and slowly descends the stairs. She's one fall away from being put in a home. The kids, even her grandchildren, relentlessly try to persuade her to leave the big house. Her accountant son, John, prepared a spreadsheet: income for the sale of the house could buy her a life of luxury in assisted living. Another son, Kenneth, put a peek hole in her door. He sells insurance. According to Kenny, a startling number of robberies result from the victim opening the door to the burglar. Well, screw that. Margaret opens the door wide enough for the whole world to enter.

There's a young man on the doorstep — she knows him. That unruly red hair, the fiery red beard, now trimmed. A goatee. Usually she finds goatees pretentious, but she likes it on Tommy, one of the prisoners who had been in the yard.

"May I help you," she asks, her voice too loud and high-pitched. No answer. She doesn't know much about him, but she does know his age from the newspaper: he's twenty.

At the age of twenty, Margaret was boringly mature. When they arrived back from the honeymoon, Walter pulled into the driveway beside the court house. Ever since she was a child, Margaret had been in awe of this gleaming white building, with its big pillars and the heavy oak doors. As a teenager, it was this building that made her dream of being a lawyer. She imagined the clacking of her high heels as she walked down the sidewalk, the important briefcase a heavy weight on her arm. She thought, This is where justice is done, and as a lawyer, Margaret would be righting society's wrongs, prosecuting the guilty and redeeming the innocent.

She sat in the car until she realized that Walter was standing beside the passenger door. He opened the door and took her hand. When she stood, facing the court house, he put his hands on her shoulders and turned her around until she was looking at the neighbouring two-storey white house.

"What do you say?" he asked.

Surely Walter wasn't thinking that they could live there. Didn't he realize that it would be torture for her to live beside the court house?

In her family, there wasn't money for education, nothing for Margaret and her four sisters, though her brother became an electrician. Margaret worked for two miserable years at the co-op store before finally accepting that she could never save enough to go to law school. Walter had wanted to be an architect but, like her, couldn't afford it. He took a job for the town as the building inspector. Drawn together by their crushed aspirations, they pledged to build a happy life of smaller goals. However, she couldn't live next to the court house. Her failure would mock her every day.

"It's too big for us," she said.

Margaret saw a flicker of dread on her new husband's face, and she realized that he'd already bought it. He would have had help from his parents. They believed in real estate, not education. He was waiting for her to be enthusiastic. She buried her face in his chest.

"We'll fill it with kids," she said, with as much vigour as she could manage. She pledged to ignore their pretentious neighbour.

They quickly filled each bedroom with children, thanks to Catholicism.

In war, the trajectory is straightforward: you identify the enemy and fight them to the death. Families are more complex. Margaret found herself in daily hand-to-hand combat with people she was required to nurture. She did not like all her children, but she knew she had to love them. The battleground was the house, especially the kitchen and the bathroom. Daily shifting loyalties. Frequent skirmishes, incidental to larger battles. Casualties on both sides. The young combatants inched forward toward the victory of leaving the house behind.

Showing up for battle every day required endless reserves of energy. There were no sick days. She felt cheated by false advertising. Magazines showed happy housewives with their feet up on the ottoman, their children sprawled across the plush carpet, watching wholesome television. The wives were shown standing in their heels and aprons, beside a gleaming stove, lipstick smiles radiating contentment. The opportunities for engagement outside the house were hollow. She did not long to volunteer for the hospital auxiliary or lust after the distinction of volunteer of the year for helping out with Welcome Wagon.

Walter thought he was doing his bit by driving them all to a cottage every summer. No hot water, no electricity, cooking meals on a wood stove. It was a vacation for him and the children loved it, but the cottage exhausted her.

She composed a poem about her own vacation:

When household tasks are endless damnation

The maternity ward is a short vacation

In the maternity ward, she would deliver the baby, and they would deliver three meals a day. As the family grew, she exaggerated her fatigue so they let her stay longer. Still, as great as it was to have a maternity ward vacation, it was short-lived and the consequences lasted a lifetime. She tried to add it up: with two babies in diapers at any given time, one poop minimum each per day times one thousand days each equals — oh, she couldn't bear to calculate it. The rhythm method obviously didn't work for them. After the miscarriages, she talked the doctor into putting her on birth control pills.

"Just to regulate your period," he said, being a Catholic like her.

After Walter had the deck built, the jail yard became even more important to Margaret. She had her puzzles to unravel, her men to ponder. Shitty bums and snotty noses were infinitely more tolerable.

Tommy wears a T-shirt. The sleeves are very short and circle tightly around his bulging biceps. Margaret may be old, but she's still a woman and she finds his muscles unbearably attractive. She forces herself to concentrate. Why is he here at her house? The newspaper hadn't divulged much about him. Margaret had pieced together the crime from the police report and other items, scattered here and there. Tommy had been charged with theft of a truck. In the classifieds, she discovered that the truck Tommy stole had been for sale: "Damaged, needs body work."

Tommy thrusts something at her. Suddenly, Margaret remembers the significance of this particular man: this is the one who looked up and saw her. Without looking down, she realizes she has taken something, something made of paper. He turns abruptly and clomps off in his heavy steel-toed boots. His body rolls forward solidly on sturdy hips under a strong back.

After despairing that the battles would never cease, unbelievably they did. The children left in fits and starts, drafted to jobs and schools in distant cities. Margaret thought, secretly, the farther away the better.

Margaret and Walter had some sacred alone time before his forgetfulness set in. Then the deck and her men regained their importance.

Walter's been in the institution these seven years. They're calling it dementia; it could be Alzheimer's, but why put him through the tests at this late stage. Margaret stopped visiting when he no longer recognized her. It was easier to think of him as dead. Someday they will tell her he is dead, mercifully and finally dead.

When her grown-up children visit, they don't knock. They walk in as if it's still their house. Margaret knows they're checking in, clocking her decline. She wants to flip on all the burners, hike up the thermostat in summer, and open the windows in winter. But her offspring are serious yuppies and they don't have her sense of humour. Now the grandchildren: they get her. They have great discussions. Doomsday book, doomsday clock — each generation inherits a prediction for imminent destruction. Perhaps they have the right solution and will fix the world's problems, perhaps not. If she's lucky, she won't be around to witness it all go poof.

When family visits, Margaret reminds them that they have to leave from three until four every afternoon. They can go for a walk or hang out at the library; she doesn't care. When they return, she lets the wives make the dinner. Or the husbands. She's retired. Margaret sees that she's holding an envelope. The fitting place to open it is the deck.

The men circle the yard, one following the other. Almost always, they smoke. As they walk the perimeter of the wall, rounding off the corners, Margaret matches each man with a crime from the police report. Usually they keep apart, alone and silent, yet she hears their excuses, feels their arrogance. Anger is rare, but when it manifests (a boot against the wall or a fist against another prisoner), her heart cheers: finally, an outlet for the pent-up emotion. Perhaps this man feels enough regret to break the cycle. Perhaps she will not see him again.

The idealism she had as a twenty-year-old is long shattered. She has lost faith in the austere court house. Lawyers and judges and jails are not dispensing justice. Sure, the men are guilty of the crimes that put them in jail. But they are innocent of the circumstances they are born into. Or they're undeserving of their misfiring body chemistry. Legal institutions — courts of law and punitive jails — don't discourage crime; they foment more illegal activity. If only her own children could appreciate their good fortune. Mothers and fathers can't be taken for granted.

From her perch, Margaret looks down at the prisoners, but she does not disdain them. The crimes, yes, but not the men. The men are her new family. She cannot right the wrongs that landed these men in jail. She can't change society or the criminal justice system. But seventy-odd years of life has taught her patience. Solutions often present themselves.

And one did.

At the drugstore, there was only one clerk on the cash. He was Margaret's least favourite person in the whole town. He spoke to old people in the same squeaky voice he used for babies.

"Oh no, Mrs. MacSween! You don't want six Mother's Day cards!"

"Yes, I do," Margaret said quietly.

"I've never sold more than one Mother's Day card to a single person. Who has more than one mother?" He chuckled.

Margaret said nothing. There were others in the store, and they were all listening. The only sound was the cards as he slid them into a brown paper bag.

"Your mother must be long dead, ha, ha," he said.

Everyone in the store collectively inhaled. Margaret calmly took the bag. In a booming voice, she said, "Sweetie, why don't you just fuck right off."

At home, she placed the Mother's Day cards inside a large manila envelope. There were six cards, one for each of the inmates at the jail at that time. She poked holes in each corner of the big envelope and threaded fine string through each hole. Then she tied all four ends of the string around a rock the size of her fist.

Everybody has a mother. Every mother deserves to be honoured. If even one mother is moved to embrace her son, if even one relationship is repaired, then her mission will be successful.

On the deck, ready for the act, Margaret's heart began an erratic dance. She remembered the stupid alarm bracelet that her kids gave her and for the first time regretted not wearing it. She willed herself to calm down. There were only two weeks before Mother's Day. She had to do this now.

When the men were all out, she threw the rock. It cleared the coil of barbed wire and sailed down into the exercise yard. It had been years since she'd thrown anything, and she wrenched her shoulder. The sudden sharp pain distracted her. Instead of ducking back out of sight, she stood there rubbing her shoulder. When she looked down, five of the men were gathered around, making Gillis suspicious. He sauntered over to see what they were up to. A prisoner slipped the package under his jacket before Gillis got there. Tommy, the youngest prisoner, glanced up. Gillis was growling threats, so Tommy pulled out a cigarette and asked for a light. That gave the others time to twist away, back into their circuit of the yard. Until that moment, Margaret was a supreme being, looking down on her subjects. These creatures were her creation, in a world of her making. Now that one saw her, they became real human beings. She hurried inside and out of sight.

For the next few weeks as she watched the men circle the yard, she wondered if any of the six had sent a card. She was comfortable not knowing.

Alone on the deck, Margaret pulled a card from the envelope. The front said Thank You in an old-fashioned font, framed by violets. Tasteful, conservative. Inside, he had printed "Thanks." No signature. No return address. And that was enough. Margaret pledged to make the cards an annual event for as long as they allowed her to live beside the court house.

PEE BREAK

Familiar spot. Favourite posture: on my back, beside the river, looking up through branches at blue sky. Willow branches. That tree I climbed when I was a boy. Lonely. I'm in the dream, too heavy to get up. Roll over.

And I'm on the river bank. Nineteen and too old to lie around under the willow. A flash of movement through the branches. Charlotte's neck, long and slender as a deer's. Flick of a white tail and she's gone. Hell, I'm still a lonely kid.

Rushing water — Sawmill Creek pouring into the Yukon River. Need to pee. Roll over. Sawmill Creek. Rushing, gushing, roaring.

Damn it! Awake now. Water leak. On my feet, down the stairs two at a time. Bare feet, dry on the carpet, then wet on the lino. In the kitchen, a waterfall pouring out of the ceiling. My hand on the switch. It flickers on. I glance up. Water streaming from the light fixture. Holy shit! I could have fried myself. Water all over the floor. Wake up, damn it. Be careful.

Pots. Bowls. The water pounding my back is hot. Strange, that the hot water pipe burst, not the cold. The containers are already full. This is not a solution. Of course — turn off the water.

The back laundry room is cold, the tap behind the set tub is rusted. I wet a rag and wrench the tap until the flow stops.

I've been awake two minutes. The pipe probably burst three minutes ago. 7:15. Too early to phone the plumber.

I helped Granddad build all the additions on his cabin. The upstairs went on, then after he moved here full time, we added the arctic entry, for insulation mostly. Final thing we added was this room at the back, for storage. All his old maps, his entire collection was in here. Where did Uncle Dryden put them? Now the walls are lined with the leftovers from the five cords of wood I'll need to see me through the winter.

He never intended to put in plumbing, and there was none for as long as he lived. He used the outhouse out back right up until he died.

"Pure folly putting running water in a log cabin," he told me.

Guess he didn't say that to Uncle Dryden. It was the first thing my uncle did when he took over the place. Winter's only halfway done. What other surprises will it spring on me? That dream of the river flowing is four months ago, and four months away.

I toss a couple of sticks of wood in the stove, small chunks so they'll burn hot and keep the pipes from freezing again.

Dawson effin' City. In the winter. How am I still in this shithole? High school was a killer, but at least it gave me an objective: to get out of Dodge. Then just before graduation, Aunt Angie begged me to take the job at the hardware store. Now and then I find something to make it tolerable — like explaining to Cheechakos why the hair dryers are in the plumbing section. But what I need is a job that will exercise my brain. Selling chainsaws and dog booties doesn't exercise any of me.

Eighteen bucks an hour — and in another three months, Angie promised to raise it forty cents. Whoopee shit.

I switch the light on in the living room. Curtains are open. And here I am, buck naked, staring out at the street. If I stand planted in this picture window long enough, I can be Dawson's biggest attraction. Word'll get around: east side of Eighth Avenue, north end. All 1,500 inhabitants can look in and laugh at me. And I don't care.

If Granddad was here to see me, he'd say, "Tu as du front tout le tour de la tête." I got my forehead all around my head. He grew up in Quebec, and these lines would just pop out of him. It means I'm stubborn — I got attitude. Well, I guess so, 'cause I'm just going to keep standing here. Self-hatred takes a lot of energy, but I'm willing to put in the effort.

When it's cold like this, the streetlights look like flying saucers. Each one of them is pulsing in the ice fog. When I was a kid, I wanted them to be alien invaders hovering over the frozen streets. They were searching for me, so they could whisk me off to another planet. Too bad they never found me.

How many beer did I drink last night? Nine. Not good, drinking alone. But who's left to drink with? The smarties from high school buggered off to college. When they came home for Christmas, they looked like friggin' hipsters. Ordered fancy-name drinks in weird glasses. What's wrong with beer?

Only go-nowheres live here now, the ones so fried by high school they settle for puny salaries and getting blasted every weekend. I don't want to hang out with any of them. Except Charlotte.

She was so cute at the hardware store, walking up to the cash yesterday with two, not one but two, extendible arm snow brushes. I never found out why she needed two. We fooled around with the sliding comfort grip. I only charged her for one, and after she paid, I invited her out to dinner. She looked around all of a sudden, and I read her — there's only one restaurant open this time of year, and everybody would see us. So I switched it to my house. She said the baby had a fever from her shot. Then I said I could bring dinner over to her place. Did I sound desperate when I said, "So we can get the baby to bed at her regular time"?

Then Aunt Angie was stomping down the aisle toward us, and Charlotte just crossed those two snow brushes in an *X* on her front, like she was a snow angel making a pledge. "Later," she said.

Then she spun around and took off. And I'm left trying to figure out how to make the sale go away 'cause Aunt Angie saw the two brushes and I only rang in one. Yup, Charlotte, I drank all that beer last night 'cause of *you*!

It was grade ten and those jerks had me against the wall, flipping lit matches at me. You stopped them. Since grade ten, I've been watching you. In grade eleven, I started wanting you. By grade twelve, I needed you. Jesus, I sound like a stalker! And I look like a flasher. Better get into some clothes.

Charlotte would like my shape. As much as I bitched about chopping wood when I was a kid, I got muscles and shoulders a girl could go for. Maybe this summer I can get Charlotte to come swimming with me. The baby will be walking by then — old enough to splash in Steamboat Sluice. Me and Charlotte sitting on the bank, holding hands, watching the baby. Just the thought of holding her hand, flesh against flesh, turns me on.

I miss Granddad. I could talk to him. Sure, he was a loner in his old age, but he always had stories for me. He was a player. He could have helped me with Charlotte.

Did Uncle Dryden tell me to leave the door to the laundry room open? I think he might have said, "When it's cold."

I scrape the frost off the kitchen window with Granddad's expired Visa card. He kept that card here by the window for years, and every time he used it, he cursed the financial giants that kept the little guys like us under their thumb.

The flashlight beam finds the outside thermometer. All the mercury is sunk down tight into the bulb. Stupid thermometer only goes to -40. Last night, before I turned in, I tried all the taps. The cold ran; the hot didn't. I spent an hour with the blow dryer thawing the pipe. Still drunk, inching the dryer along, like I was tracing my heritage: Granddad to my dad and down to me.

There can't be many young guys like me, nineteen years old and I want to have kids. I would buy this place and add a couple of bedrooms. Too bad Granddad never made a will. I'm pretty sure he would have left the place to me. How'd I let myself get into this mess, paying Uncle Dryden sixty percent of my income? I need a giant credit card to scrape him outta my life. Damn him and his amateur plumbing. He better not expect me to pay for the repair.

Time to phone Gord Harvey now.

He says, "I'll send a plumber over soon as he shows up."

Plumber? If Gord's not coming, then it won't be a plumber — he's the only one in town.

Red Dead Redemption is beating me bad when there's a bang on the door. He's already in the arctic entry when I open the inside door. Balaclava, fur hat on top, scarf. Only the eyes are exposed, and I don't know it's him until I hear, "Hey, Craig."

Gord's son Lance is the last person I want to see. Bastard stands there, door still open behind him, a cloud of condensed air rolling in and swirling all around us.

He won't move until I tell him to. "Close the door and come in, Lance."

The tool box shakes the floor when he lets it drop. He peels out of his heavy gear by the wood stove. The stove kicks off so much heat that Lance makes a dig about how someone must be really screwed up to have a pipe burst in a house this hot.

I tell him, "Uncle Dryden put in the plumbing himself. He should have hired the only professional plumber in town — your father."

Lance is not smart but he catches on and he states his case: he's been an apprentice for years; he would have his papers if there was anybody in this shithole who could certify him. Soon as he's not so busy, he'll go down to Whitehorse to get certified, but he's looking at the spring now 'cause of all the stupid people who don't know how to keep their pipes from busting.

I pop a beer. When I offer it to Lance, he turns it down.

"Nine a.m.," he points out, like I don't know what time it is.

There's not a lot of space for the two of us and a tool box in the laundry room. While I call the hardware store, Lance deliberately bangs the pipe.

After I hang up, he says, "Why call in sick? This won't take long."

That does it. I tell him, "Ready to hear what you should do?"

"Listen, buddy," Lance says. "If this is about Charlotte, I give her money every month."

I step in closer, crowding him. "You think this is about money? That baby is yours."

He shoves me back. "That baby's none of your business. Charlotte's none of your business," he says.

"Charlotte is my business. She's my friend."

He picks up a huge pipe wrench, toss it back and forth, one hand to the other.

"Hey, I get it," he says. "You want Charlotte to be more than your friend, right?" He turns and examines the burst pipe. "Never gonna happen. She don't date losers."

Lance is taller than me, but he's skinny. I pull out the biggest pipe wrench. I push forward. I pin him with the wrench under his chin, flatten him up against the wall. He sputters and struggles, but I hold him tight.

Now I'm shouting. "She's got a lot of problems, but you're the biggest one. She doesn't know you don't give a shit. You're just stringing her on!"

For a skinny guy, Lance has a lot of muscle. He twists free. Suddenly I'm on the floor, wedged between the washing machine and the legs of the sink. He's on my chest. He bangs my hand against the washer until I drop the wrench. I try to buck him off, but he's got me pinned good.

I yell, "Do you ever look at the baby? Her smile is her mother's, but when she cries, she looks like you!"

Lance punches me in the face. It hurts, and as I blink up at him, I see he's surprised too. He rolls off.

I sit up and check my face — my nose is bleeding. I find a rag. Lance digs in his tool box and bangs things around.

I get the second last beer and open it. When I hold it out, Lance's face contorts, and I watch as his contempt softens into something else.

I tell him, "It's okay, it's after nine."

He takes the bottle and drinks almost the whole thing in one gulp. After I wipe my face, I stand against the wall and watch him replace the section of pipe and close it back up. It takes about an hour.

While he gets into his cold weather gear, I check the wood stove. From the wood box, I pull out a gnarly chunk, the top of a spruce with cones. I hold it up before tossing it in.

"Wood and kindling combined," I say.

Lance makes a harrumphing sound, then opens the door, and I think that's going to be it.

This guy likes to stand in open doorways. He's so covered up that he's almost not there. His words come muffled from behind the balaclava.

"I'll tell her."

I stand in the open doorway, watching him walk away. Lance becomes a ghost floating in the ice fog until he disappears. The sun won't hit this part of town for another few weeks, but a pink and purple light bruises the sky to remind you where the east is. The hot air around me lifts and collides with the cold, manifesting as a swirling white cloud. I take a deep breath. The air hurts. Lungs can freeze at this temperature. I want the air to hurt, and it does as I pull it deep inside me.

There's still one beer left, and I drink it slowly. I've been in love with Charlotte for a few years. I'll give her a few months to get over Lance. I'll offer dinner again, see if she needs anything done around the apartment. Granddad would say, "Tu vas vite sur tes patins." You're fast on your skates. And I am. I'll start now, whittling something for the baby. A toy boat. One day in the spring, I'll take them to Sawmill Creek, sit on the bank. When it warms up enough, we'll go swimming at Steamboat Sluice.

THE DRUNK STRANGER

At first I think it's a burlap bag. Then I make out a brown sweater with crispy orange and red maple leaves stuck to it. The night is foggy and moonless, so I stand over the lump and force my eyes to decipher the parts. A knee is sticking up, and an elbow. The realization that it is a body startles me, but I'm not afraid. I can just hear the nuns lecturing me: a young woman must not walk alone at night, certainly not in a rowdy port like Lunenburg, and she absolutely must not halt on a deserted path. In defiance of the voices, I continue to study the body.

This is not one of my neighbours. I know them all by sight if not by name. There are two distinct categories: the masters, and those who serve them. I belong to the latter.

A sudden snore. I spring back. This is not a dead body.

"Are you all right?" The lump doesn't stir. I poke it with the pointed toe of my boot. "Hello?"

A grunt. The limbs untangle. The elbow unfolds into an arm, the knee into a long leg. Then the other leg and arm, as if rousing from a deep slumber. A man manifests on the gravel path, a perfectly formed human with a mass of curly hair. His eyelids open slowly. He blinks twice.

I am surprised to see that he is young. Men his age are rare because the Great War claimed so many. But then the war has been over for five years now. Probably this lucky youth had been too young to go overseas.

The temperature is below freezing and will drop several more degrees before dawn. I can't leave him lying here all night.

"May I help you to your feet?" I ask.

He twists his head up to get a better look at me. "May I? *May* I?"

There is mockery in his voice.

I have been mocked for much of my twenty years, by my fellow residents in the orphanage and by the nuns. Now I endure the ridicule of the family I work for — the judge, his wife, and on down to the youngest of their children. I've learned to decipher the intent of each taunt. They seek to establish their supremacy and reinforce my diminutive status. This young man is confused because my clothes and demeanour indicate that I'm serving class, yet I speak proper English. And I am confused by him: he is not dressed modestly enough to be in service, yet his clothing, although of good quality, doesn't proclaim wealth. He is slender and clean-shaven and looks healthy enough. Better turned out than a stevedore but not as fancy as a sea captain.

When I don't respond to his taunt, his face breaks into a grin.

"You may," he answers, holding up his arm.

I take a firm hold and watch as he extends, limb by limb, like one of those hinged wooden measuring sticks. When he's upright, I judge him to be over six feet. He sways, so I grab him around the waist. He swings his arm around my shoulder, a damp weight that makes me realize how seldom I have felt a body — any body — this close to mine. At the orphanage, the Sisters of Mercy fiercely protected their virgin girls. Their Halifax convent was a fortress. The nuns took in young women who were "in trouble," nursed them through childbirth, then raised the babies in the orphanage. A few lucky children were adopted. Those who weren't adopted had their rough edges sanded down and their wills curtailed so that they funnelled nicely into religious orders. The girls became nuns, and the boys, priests. Those whose spirits couldn't be broken were spit out into humble positions, like me, a domestic working for little more than room and board.

The stranger looks at me with an expression of innocence, surprised to find me beneath his outstretched arm. The smell coming off him puts me in mind of the brewery on the dock. I ask his name.

"Nothing but trouble, my name," he says, and then doesn't tell me. Instead: "Yours?"

My inclination is to reveal nothing, but I fear that if I don't engage him, he might bolt into the dark. Countless men died of hypothermia during the war. If he were to freeze to death here in the woods, his young life will be on my conscience forever. So I tell him a half-truth.

"I'm Amy." What does it matter? I won't ever see him again.

Now the question is what to do with him. My attic room in the judge's house is nearby, but it won't do. Men are not allowed in my apartment — that was made clear when I was taken on. Even if it were allowed, I would not have the strength, and he would not have the sobriety for the long climb up the outside staircase.

"I'll help you home. Where do you live?"

His only reply is a dismissive snort.

I love my apartment because for the first time in my life, I have a place of my own. Upon entering one sees the single bed. There is a wardrobe with my four dresses and coat, and a window with a cracked pane. This time of year, the wind lifts the spray off the harbour and flings it against the house, driving the damp into my bones. All winter I shiver, and in the summer there's no relief from the stagnant heat.

My only other home was the orphanage, where for sixteen years I endured the sorrow of other sad souls. I was tainted by the sight and smell of their misery. In my new life, for six days a week, I am in service. Sunday is mine, and in the privacy of my room, I plot my escape from this life of servitude. Until recently, that is.

I ask the stranger, more insistently this time, where he lives. He mumbles about a boarding house on Kissing Bridge Road. I know the street and it's only five blocks away, but unfortunately uphill. I turn him around, toward Kaulbach Street. With my arm around his waist and his arm still heavy across my shoulders, our progress is slow. Suddenly he decides he doesn't like standing up, so he twists out of my grip and slumps down to the gravel sidewalk.

Under the streetlight, I'm surprised to see he's a redhead — like me. There is an unfair assumption that redheads are stubborn. When he looks up at me, drunkenly defiant, I conclude that stubborn is accurate in his case. Am I stubborn too?

The nuns did not hold back about having been "chosen." They talked frequently and with fervour about their call to religious service. God Himself told them they had a vocation to be His handmaids. What greater mission than to care for "fallen angels" and their unwanted children? When I grew impervious to their calling, they labelled me a stubborn redhead.

Girls who are marked by childhood illness don't get adopted. But if we survive to our teen years, we earn a cubicle with a window. From my dorm window on the top floor, I could see the university through the treetops. Like a holy city in a distant land, the imposing clock tower summoned me. My vocation was not to serve God. I was intended for university to study medicine and repair people like me who have been impeded by bad health.

I took to sneaking into the orphanage library to study biology and anatomy. There were few books that were useful, but I devoured them. In the orphanage clinic, I found a hiding place in a closet in the operating theatre. I witnessed half a dozen births before the nuns discovered me. Pressured to disclose my intention, I told them I was destined to be a doctor. If only they had ridiculed me. But no, it was pity they doled out to the stubborn redhead. Did I not realize that girls don't go to university and almost all doctors are men? Certainly a girl like me, with a deformation, could not have a career. They accused me of reaching beyond my station in life. On the other hand, they said, a healthy orphan had a few options: if she could come up with funding to be trained, she could be a nurse or a teacher. But a girl like me — with legs bowed by rickets — the nuns said they would be grateful to find someone to take me into service. Despite being top of my class, the nuns discouraged my scholastic ambitions. Their concession was to allow me to attend grade nine, but as soon as I completed it, they presented me with a small, battered suitcase. With all my belongings inside, it was still quite empty. My three favourite nuns hustled me outside onto the grand steps. I was especially fond of Sister Marie Joseph, younger than the others and still no chin hairs. They instructed me to take the train to Lunenburg, find the judge's house, and give him their letter of recommendation.

My knees shook as I walked away. Except for an occasional excursion, I had never been outside the grounds. Before the gate I turned, hoping to see in their faces a reflection of the sadness I felt at our parting. All three smiled broadly. They waved at me. When I was just outside the gate, I turned again, but they had already returned inside. I was yet one more orphan, an egg they had kept warm until maturity. Then they pierced me at both ends and blew me out into the world.

Working for the judge has been miserable. The daily tasks are mindless and demeaning, but that's not the worst of it. The judge pays me a monthly pittance and then extracts an exorbitant portion for room and board. Every payday, he expects me to express my gratitude. Is he naturally arrogant, or did the nuns groom him to treat me as if I have no other options?

I have been frugal, forbidding myself luxuries — even necessities — to save every penny. After a full three years of service, I forced myself to do the calculations. The projection is dismal: by the time I have enough money for university, I will be thirty-six years old!

Of all the disappointments so far, this is the cruellest. I must settle for a life of menial labour. The nuns accurately predicted my destiny, though if we were to cross paths, I would not admit to them that they were right.

When my friend Annie, a governess, invited me to her rooming house to consult the Ouija board, I eagerly accepted. The nuns condemn talking boards and parlour games, saying they lead to demonic possession. Now I go out of my way to do the opposite of what they preach. Dabble in the occult? Yes, that's for me.

Annie asked the Ouija the name of the man she'll marry. Our fingers rested lightly on the planchette. It flew across the board and pointed to Good Bye. She asked how long she'd wait to meet him and how many children she'd have, and received the same answer. Poor Annie accused me of pushing the planchette. My honest reply was that I did not.

I asked the Ouija about my mother. At the orphanage, that question was forbidden. We were admonished for concocting visions of loving mothers. According to the Sisters of Mercy, our mothers did not love us. They were wicked sinners, punished by their pregnancies. They cared nothing for their babies. If it weren't for the good nuns, we would have been abandoned and left to die.

When I hid in the operating theatre, I witnessed the cruelty of the nursing nuns. The poor girls talked of rape and incest, but the nuns didn't believe their stories. During the births when they were trapped in their terrible pain, no mercy was shown. Mothers and offspring had the same status on the bottom rung of the social ladder. We were like the frayed hem of a robe, dragging in the dirt.

Three times I asked the talking board, "Will I meet my mother?" Twice it pointed to GOOD BYE, GOOD BYE. The third time, it spelled out "B-O-Y."

After the Ouija experience, I am in the mood to solve mysteries. Who is this young man I have found? I can tell he has not been tainted by life's disappointments. Perhaps he has glimpsed them, but his aspirations have not been crushed as mine have. As I walk him up the hill, I doggedly ask questions. His story comes out in fits and starts.

He arrived in town just a day ago. He is in search of his family.

I ask, "How can you have family and not know where they are?"

"That's what they said, those fellows in the tavern. They thought I was a rumrunner. Look at me — do I look like I smuggle rum? Do I sound like a Frenchman from Miquelon?"

I know little about Frenchmen and Miquelon. The young man before me looks to be of Celtic origin, Scottish or Irish. Perhaps he is an apprentice — something sophisticated like boat design?

He switches direction suddenly, heading down the hill. I wrestle him around, so we don't end up in the harbour. He proclaims adamantly that his mission is to find "her." In the forefront of my mind is "mother." When I ask, he shakes his head.

"Your aunt, then? Grandmother?"

"They kept it from me. They decided to tell me when I turned twenty. My parents! Ha! Turns out they're not my parents. They're my adoptive parents."

I am suddenly more interested in the man whose arm is such a heavy weight on my shoulders. Like me, he had a mother who gave him up. Unlike me, he was chosen. I spent my childhood watching the chosen leave. I stood at the window with the others, staring. The unwanted witnessing the liberation of the wanted. After each adoption, there was bedwetting, there were fights. Precious personal possessions were stolen or destroyed. The nuns served us cake to celebrate the adoption, they said. As the years passed and parents passed me by, cake was not sufficient comfort. I find myself less patient with this drunk stranger. No, not impatient — resentful.

We have arrived at Kissing Bridge Road. I assume the young man recognizes the street so I push his arm away. He takes the lead, but after two blocks, he stops. He looks around, shakes his head. With a dazed look on his face, he plops down onto the ground and blinks.

Neither of us has the energy to continue. We need a break.

Because I am curious, as always, about who birthed him, I ask, "Did you find your mother, your real mother?"

He looks up at me from the dirt sidewalk. "My father — the man who adopted me — said she worked for a fish merchant. That merchant took her, while she was still a girl. My father saw she was pregnant and got her out of there. Gave her to the nuns."

"And?" I ask.

"They who won't tell me anything about her. I gave up on her. Like she gave up on me."

He groans loudly and leans back. In the streetlight, I study him top to bottom, from the smart haircut to the fine leather shoes. I am reminded of the nuns and their cruelty. The new mothers pleaded to hold their babies, even to keep them, but they were denied.

My impatience with this lad turns to anger. I want to get rid of him. I pull him to his feet.

He wobbles so I grab him firmly by the waist again. I point us up Kissing Bridge Road again.

"You have no right to be angry at your mother."

"It's because of my mother that I was tormented. The boys at school tormented me. It started the first day of school and continues to this day. Because of her whimsy."

"What could she have possibly done?"

He raises his arms in an exasperated gesture. "She named me Jasper. Why such a stupid name?"

This young man complains about such a trivial thing! He was chosen: he can do whatever he fancies. He can get a decent job, pick any trade or save for university. Now I want to slap his face.

He mumbles, "All I could find out was that before she moved to Halifax, before her position with the fish merchant, she had lived in Joggins. There are gems on the beaches there, and semi-precious stones. She named her babies after them."

I stop dead. "She had more than one?"

"Me and my twin," he says.

I see the planchette flying across the Ouija board: B-O-Y. I am grateful for the darkness as I feel my face flush. I feel fury rising from the soles of my feet.

"How could they separate the twins? Why didn't they adopt the girl too?"

Jasper realizes I've stopped. He stops too. "Hey, you're right! My twin is a girl. Those nuns are some mean with their information. Except this young one, when she showed me out, she let it slip. Lunenburg. And a name: Amethyst."

I feel like I'm caught in a heavy surf. A wave pushes me forward toward the beach; another pulls me back into the depths. I stare at Jasper, my redheaded brother, and I pulse with love and hate and anger and regret. I feel the bond of our shared mother and the sorrow of years lost. I am unable to get up safely to the beach without another wave rolling over me and knocking me down. And another wave and another.

When Jasper speaks again, his voice is subdued. "If she hates her name as much as I hate Jasper, odds are she doesn't go by that."

He looks around him, and for the first time all night, there's a glimmer of recognition in his eyes. He points rigidly to a large house with a sign that reads Kissing Bridge Lodge. I follow him around to the back entry. He turns to me just before pulling the door open.

"Those fellas in the tavern were no help at all."

I watch until the door closes behind him. There is a loud clatter as if he's knocked over a fry pan. I wait and watch until on the second floor a light goes on and shines out a small window. I feel the cold now, but I'm unable to move. That light goes off and soon another comes on, spilling through a bigger window.

After the nuns ridiculed my aspirations to be a doctor, I was inconsolable. Sister Marie Joseph tried to comfort me. She broke the rules and told me that my mother became a problem for them when she refused to leave without me. Sister Superior finally conceded, and they made an agreement. My mother was permitted to keep me for as she long as she was breastfeeding. So she stayed on, caring for her baby as the pregnant women came and went. I was three years old before my mother gave me over to the orphanage. Even she could see that I had rickets.

I had studied up on my ailment in medical journals I found in the clinic. In one of them was a groundbreaking discovery: the most common cause of rickets is a vitamin D deficiency. The study found "this can result from exclusive breastfeeding without vitamin D supplementation."

The light in the lodge window goes out. Jasper has settled down for the night. I keep watch as I work out a strategy. He did not reveal how long he intends to stay in Lunenburg, so tomorrow morning I will come early before he can leave.

I will introduce myself to my brother. (In the event, he remembers me from tonight, it will be a reintroduction.) I will state my resolve to never lie to my brother. All our lives, we have been lied to. His parents waited until July 15 to tell him he was adopted. I was deceived by the nuns. Until tonight, I thought Sister Marie Joseph was a friend — but she didn't tell me I have a twin.

Before I see Jasper again, I must forgive my mother for causing me to have rickets. I cannot prejudice Jasper against her for an innocent mistake. Also, I have to accept that he was adopted while I was left behind. I may, however, sling a few barbs at him for the opportunities he's enjoyed. I'll make fun of him because he can't hold his liquor. And I can mock his stupid name. Because isn't that what siblings do, tease and torment each other?

THE SOLUTION FOR SLEEPLESSNESS

I woke up. It was the middle of the night, and I couldn't get back to sleep. I had been at a dinner party where Blaise had boasted about his surefire solution for sleeplessness.

"I get out of bed. I go to the coldest place in the house, and I sit there until I'm really cold. I sleep naked so I sit there starkers until I got goosebumps. Then I go back and crawl into that nice bed. I warm up and fall asleep."

So I decided to try Blaise's technique. I got out of bed. The wood stove was well stoked, the logs blazing, so the house wasn't cold enough. I stepped into my slippers and went outside. I stood there naked in the yard. It was early fall, and there was just enough snow to reflect the moonlight. Nobody was around. A dog came trotting along, sniffing at the frozen vegetation on the edge of the street. When he spotted me standing in the yard, he stopped. He stared at me long enough for me to worry he might attack. Then he threw back his head and howled like a sled dog. When I still didn't move, he bolted back the way he came.

It didn't seem cold enough in the yard, so I went through the gate to the street. A boy came walking along, eight or nine years old. He was swinging a large brown paper bag. He didn't seem to have a care in the world. What was he doing up in the middle of the night? Could he be sleepwalking? I waved to him, beckoning him to me. He clutched his bag to his chest and stared at me. When I approached, he spun around and ran away.

I crossed Front Street and climbed up the dike. The fresh snowfall had made the slope slippery. When I made it to the top, my eyes were drawn to a flickering light down by the shore. The river wasn't frozen yet, and I walked toward the light. As I drew closer, I saw down below, by the river, a huge bonfire. People circled the fire, chanting. I realized they were all women. They were dressed in long white robes, and they held hands.

I watched from the top of the dike. Were they a coven of witches? I didn't want to disturb them, but I needed to know if my body was cold enough yet. One of the younger ones left the group. With her gloved hands, she lifted her long white robe so she could see her feet as she climbed the dike. She was as nimble as a caribou. When she reached the top, I held out my arms in greeting, as if to embrace her. She stopped.

I said, "Am I cold enough? Do I have goosebumps?"

She stared at me for a moment before she slowly nodded her head. Was she nodding because I had goosebumps, or did I block her way? I turned and left her there. I walked back down the dike, across Front Street, and along to my house. I climbed into bed.

I woke shivering. The fire needed to be stoked. This time, throwing off the blankets worked just fine. But some night I'd like to try Blaise's technique. It could be an adventure.

SPLINTER AND SHARD

Weird. I'm against the ceiling, looking down. I've always known about this. Like, when I blow things up. Light the fuse, back away. Tingle, wait, wait. BOOM! Solids become particles. Things go back to the way they were, tiny bits of matter in space. It all comes down to this: me, in tiny bits.

What's that? Smoke detector? No, it's Bronwyn. She's wailing. She's looking at me — that bloody mess that is me. They're crowding in now, nurses with their open arms. Arms around Bronwyn, they pull her away. Yes, get her out of here!

Calls. Alarms. Machines wheeled in. A team around the body on the bed, leaning in, trying to bring me back. A tug of war, them pulling on their end of the rope, and me pulling on mine, leaning back with all my weight. Hey, Dad, you pulling with me?

Bronwyn with the Crazy Grin. I loved calling her that. A teacher. Pretty. Educated. The Boys couldn't believe it.

"What the fuck?"

Even the guy at rehab. "You got something going for you, Sean, to get a girl like that."

We met at the Last Call. I came in the door and saw a blond at the bar. She was trying to cover up how hot she was with a blouse buttoned to the neck and a big white bow at the top, unsexy pants. She was with a couple of straight guys, one a nerd and the other a jock. Perfectly trimmed beards. Turned out they were new teachers. The blond was being nice, having a friendly drink to welcome them to the school. And my friends, the Boys — Arnie and Buddy — were sitting at the bar too.

I stood there pretending to let my eyes adjust while I tried to figure out how to explain myself to Arnie and Buddy. Two chicks were huddled over a table near the bar. In the corner, I saw a booth full of girls hiding out. From the way they glanced up at me and looked away, I could tell they knew about me and Arnie and Buddy and were staying clear. How could I break it to the Boys that I didn't want to play their game anymore. They'd done so much for me. I was a seventeen-year-old fuck-up when they took me on and trained me in munitions. I made mistakes: they rescued me from some tight spots. They initiated me in their private sport, and now I had to tell them I was done.

The Boys have a name for it: Dip the Wick and Switch the Bitch. We'd enter a party or a bar, haul out our cellphones, and start the stopwatch. The first to swing their feet up off the floor onto a bed would stop the timer. He would text out a screengrab of the stopwatch. Whoever got laid the quickest won. Next time we got together, the losers bought drinks for the winner. Girls were like rabbits: we would track 'em down and coax 'em to a bed. Any bed. Ugly bed. Dirty sheets. Nothing stuck, no residue. An eyelash on a pillow — blow it away.

Looking at the Boys there at the bar that night, I could see they had worked out a strategy. Arnie would put the moves on the blond, and Buddy was his backup. I had just worked up the nerve to tell them when this short redhead intercepted me, popped up right in front of me. I recognized her: was it only a week since I'd picked her up? It felt like a lifetime ago — I wasn't that pitiful asshole anymore. I was ashamed of that me. Now she was in my face, earnest: "There's this party, see . . ." and did I want to go with her? I made an excuse. What was wrong with her that she thought she couldn't do better than me? Then she said she had an extra ticket for a concert. I kept shifting to see around her, so I could watch how it was playing out at the bar. Arnie shouldered in, separating the blond from the two guys. The music was too loud to hear, but I knew the routine. Arnie offered her a drink; she turned him down. He ordered one anyway. He threw his arm over her shoulder. His hand brushed her breast, as if it were an accident.

The two guys with her got twitchy. That's when Buddy took over. He yelled, reared back, grabbed his head like he was in pain. He held that pose until they asked what was wrong. He curled back his upper lip and showed them the gap. I'd never seen him use the tooth before. The distraction used to be the scar that sliced his forehead in two. He made up a different story every time about how he got the scar. I wished I could hear what he was saying about his tooth — I'd pulled it out on our last bender. While he had their attention, the drink arrived and Arnie gave it to the blond and clinked her glass. The blond tolerated Arnie until he darted in for a kiss, then she wiggled away. The guys caught on and wham, it was the Boys against the newbies. Shoving. Yelling. Fists in the air. I sidestepped the redhead and went right up to the blond. I looked her right in the eye and told her, "We gotta get you out of here." That's all I did — well, I did more than that. I took her arm and led her out. And that's how she got the idea I'm a good guy, that I protect.

That first night with her all we did was talk. We didn't even touch each other, just walked all over town for hours, yacking about whatever came up. I wasn't in the habit of doing that. The Boys taught me that if you keep up the physical assault, you can avoid intimacy because that's what chicks wanted and intimacy was a weakness. When I dropped Bronwyn off at her apartment, she hinted about getting together again, and I thought, Friends okay, not lovers. She was a teacher, for Christ's sake. Then the next night, a light tapping on my apartment door. She just happened to find out where I lived and she had a loaf of bread, still warm. The next time, I didn't answer. She yelled through the window, "I baked too many cookies." Then I started listening for her knock. That pissed me off royally. When she showed up with a whole cake, icing on it and ice cream, I opened the door, but I wouldn't let her in.

"You can't change me" is what I said.

She told me that at school when she did the unit on bullying with her students, she had me in mind. She said she knew that I was a good man. Seriously? I should have told her about me and the Boys right then, but I was too chickenshit. She said she couldn't help herself — she was falling for me. She teared right up, looked like a little girl. What could I do? She'd found the crack in my cement and poked her finger in.

Then we started sleeping together. What I liked most was when our legs wrapped around each other like braided wire, twisted together to shield against electromagnetic interference. We were stronger together. But then one evening, she was at my place and we were cooking dinner, music playing, we were so happy, and Arnie and Buddy walked in. Didn't even knock. They laid a two-four and a forty pounder of vodka on the table and dropped a bag of pot on a plate. They were edgy because I'd been ignoring their calls. Who was more surprised, the Boys or Bronwyn?

Buddy said, "No dinner for me, Sean. Don't wanna dull the buzz."

They plunked themselves in chairs. I looked at Bronwyn, and I could see her unravelling from me. She grabbed her jacket and was out the door. I caught up to her outside.

"How could you?" she said. "Did you just forget to mention that those hustlers are your friends?"

I knew all the excuses in the world couldn't save me. I let her leave, gave her a week, then I invited her out. She said no. I promised it would be a date she would never forget. I told her not to worry about a hard hat; I had an extra one.

I drove her to the dump. The whole way there, sitting beside me in the truck, Bronwyn was as impenetrable as a steel vault. The gate was locked with a heavy chain, but I'd brought all my tools. There was no way I was going to fuck this up. I got out my bolt cutter and handed her the flashlight — that way she was an accomplice right off — and I snapped the chain. I led her to where the flattened cars were piled on top of each other, and I wired up the two tallest stacks. She knew I did demolitions, but she needed to see it, to feel it.

When I was set to blast off the first one, I asked, "You ready?"

Bronwyn slid behind me and flattened up against my back. She was scared of shock waves, but I told her there wouldn't be any.

"This is subsonic combustion," I told her.

Then I blew those cars sky-high. I asked her if she wanted to set off the second explosion, and she did. She was trembling when she put her hand on the detonator. All that hot metal shot up into the air, and the look on her face — I saw that, like me, she was in awe of the power and humbled at the same time. I knew then there was a chance I could get her back.

I took her hand, and we raced out of there before the cops came. I got as much speed out of that old truck as I could. I turned down a dirt road and drove us far from town to a mine site. We sat on a tailings pile to decompress with a bottle of white wine. Wine is her preference, not mine, but I was counting on getting at the vodka when we went back to my place. I described my work, how here in the Yukon it was mostly mining, blasting cliffs. I told her about deflagration and conflagration and detonation. You don't need to go to school to learn this stuff; you don't need to be a certified demolitions engineer to get hired. Arnie and Buddy aren't certified, but they taught me everything I need to know about binary explosives and boosters and ANFO and TNT and all the letters. It was thanks to them I had a career. I told Bronwyn that when they were training me, I made mistakes, and if it weren't for them, I'd be dead now.

"In my line of work, you get careless you could get blown to smithereens," I told her.

Playing up the danger worked. She asked me about this scar and that, but not one scar was from blasting. It was embarrassing. Most of the scars were from fighting. Even worse she asked about the ones from when I was drunk and put my fist through a wire mesh window. The more honest I was, the more I was afraid that I'd drive her away. But I could feel our individual wires braiding together again. I was back in the teacher's good books.

I let Bronwyn make plans for our future. Marriage. She asked me! I said yes. Never loved a woman before. There was nothing I wouldn't do for her. When we talked about having children, she said she couldn't give up teaching for long — she loved those kids at school. When they were learning to read, she lived for the moment of revelation when they grasped that the marks on the page made sounds and that sounds became words and those words told a story.

Bronwyn pissed me off when she said I had a learning disability. My whole life people told me I was stupid; I didn't need to hear it from her too. Then she explained she meant I was the opposite of stupid. It's the smart people who often go undiagnosed, she said. She figured I had dyslexia and she's trained to teach people like me. Maybe, she thought, I could have another problem too, AD-blah-blah. I'd tease her something fierce about that — the AD-whatever.

"Can't remember all the letters 'cause of my disability," I'd say.

She laughed and pointed out that I remembered the ones I needed to remember, like TNT.

The trouble with demolitions, it's not steady. There was a lot of downtime. When I wasn't working, that's when I got in trouble. I drank heavy for half my life, since I was thirteen years old. She could see how the alcohol was a real problem.

I told her, "My dad drank till he died. Grandpa too; died young. I got those genes."

At first Bronwyn thought she could love it out of me. One part love in, equal part alcohol out. Too bad it doesn't work that way. My mother tried, and she stuck it out with Dad until I was fifteen. I didn't blame her when she moved out. She hung around town until my father drank himself to death, then she moved down south. We text and call, but we haven't seen each other for two years.

Doing rehab again was my idea, not Bronwyn's. The other two times I'd had no anchor. Now I was hard-wired to someone. When I got out, Bronwyn made it her cause to teach me to read. The way she taught, it started to make sense. I learned fast, she said, because I was intelligent. News to me. I hit the books hard, just to impress her. She said she would help me find a steady job. I was on the path. Third time lucky.

Then not so lucky. The rehab succeeded, but the body failed. When Bronwyn found out about the appointment with the oncologist, she said, "We're going to get through this together, Sean O'Flanagan."

The moment she said that I knew I was in trouble. Not the *this* (the cancer), the *together*. I didn't want her getting dragged down with me.

At the appointment, we got all the gory details. Cancer of the bowel, removal of the cancer, temporary colostomy. After treatment, reattach the plumbing. There's a higher incidence of this kind of cancer in alcoholics. Bronwyn asked the questions I was scared to ask, about changing the bag, controlling the odour. She took my hand and asked about sex.

"Because we're planning on having a family," she said. That's when I pulled my hand out of hers. Then she said, "As soon as all this settles down."

All this didn't settle. While I waited for the surgery, my condition changed. Bronwyn complained I was more intimate with the toilet than I was with her. I held on as long as I could 'cause I didn't want to scare her. Finally, I told her, "I'm passing blood," but I knew it was worse than that. Emergency trip to the hospital. Sunday afternoon. They stuck me in a room. In the morning, they'd figure it out.

It was me and Bronwyn and two empty beds and white walls. A goddamn clock hung up high. Big as an extra-large pizza. Noisy as a cannon in a glass box. Bang, bang, bang — more seconds of my wasted life pounded by.

I kept having to drag myself to the can to let it go. I got so weak, I passed out and fell off the toilet. When I came to, I heard her banging on the door. I wouldn't unlock it. I wouldn't let her see all my shit and blood. I told her, "Get a nurse." But there was another door to the bathroom, from the room next door. She found me, and she freaked out. I heard her yelling as I passed out again.

I never expected to live long. All my heroes died young. When I was a teenager, I wanted a belt buckle that said "Burn bright and die young."

The night of the tooth — no, actually it was morning — Arnie and Buddy and me were having a rough landing, coming down off X or H or MDA. (See, I can't keep these letters straight.) Buddy had a toothache. For days, he was dulling it with tequila. Guess that stopped working. That morning he grabbed a pipe wrench from his tool kit.

"Pull it out," he said, handing it to me.

Like a snarling dog, Buddy drew back his lip. His front tooth was black at the root. I knew that tooth. I was there when it'd been loosened in a fight.

My aunt, the dental hygienist, told me stuff about teeth, like how acid indigestion can cause decay and how smoking is bad for your teeth. I told him he should see a dentist, that he could get a root canal or a cap or something.

"Fuck it," Buddy said. "It's not like I'm gonna live much longer." When you don't expect to get old, you don't care about a hole in your smile.

Then Arnie said, "Yep, me too."

Shit. All three of us believed we'd die young. Here, in a country with so much going for it that people are desperate to get in. We had good bodies, education, opportunities. Sure, our work in demolitions was dangerous, but it wasn't the work that would kill us. We were bent on killing ourselves. I got mad at myself and at them for squandering it all. I crawled over to Buddy, and I took that wrench. I got a good hold on his head, and I yanked that tooth out.

After that, I was different. I looked at time as something to live, not kill. And I was done with playing their screwing game.

When I came to, I wasn't in the bathroom anymore. I was in bed and there were nurses fussing over me. They had me between the sheets now and had taken my clothes. They were putting a gown on me, the ones that make you feel less than human.

Bronwyn left the room with the doctor. In the hall, they had one of those hushed conversations, just loud enough that you think you can hear but you can't. *He* this and *his* that. Bronwyn came back in, and she talked to me in a voice pitched too high, like I was one of the kids she teaches.

"The doctor says they'll do emergency surgery first thing tomorrow morning."

Then that line again: "We're going to get through this together, Sean O'Flanagan."

I felt a prick and looked at my arm and saw a nurse putting an IV in me. The nurse said I was dehydrated, and she was giving me fluids and something for the pain. I waited until we were alone before I spoke to Bronwyn.

"I'm too far gone for a temporary, right?"

She didn't answer, just patted my hair as if I were a duck with ruffled feathers.

"I'll be shitting in a bag for the rest of my life, right?"

Since that night at the dump, we had been straight with each other. Now she wouldn't answer me.

Whatever the nurse gave me was wrapping me in a warm blanket. I needed to get the goods, now.

"Right?" I asked.

"They can tell us more after the surgery." Her voice was quivery. "After the surgery, the cancer will be all gone."

I could see she was scared too.

She said, "Then we can get back on track with our plans."

Bronwyn tried to smile. Moved in close. Big brown eyes. My eyes found that faint blue vein on the edge of her forehead. I watched it glow beneath her pale skin. Then I was floating on a warm sea. I rolled over and peered down through the murky waters. There on the ocean floor was a blue sea snake. It pushed into the golden sand and came out again, over and over. I was the sand. I could feel the light touch of the snake sliding across my chest, into my navel and out again. I realized she, Bronwyn, was the snake. That's when I knew how much I loved her. I loved that faint blue vein.

I pulled myself up out of the sea. She wasn't beside me anymore. She was over by the window, facing the dark night outside. Her shoulders were shaking, and I realized she was having one of those hard cries where your whole body empties out.

The total sum of my life: I smashed lots of cars. Set magnificent fires. Blew up tons of shit. I had a proficiency for destruction. In high school, I was the career counsellor's favourite challenge. Every time I'd make an honest effort, the booze would sabotage me. It didn't matter shit when it was only me dealing with the consequences.

I looked at the woman crying by the window. "Bronwyn?"

When she took her time responding, I knew it was so I wouldn't see how upset she was. She came over to me, holding her head up.

"I'm staying the night," she said. She plunked down on the bed beside me. She slid one hand inside her turquoise cowboy boot and pulled her foot out, careful not to chip her red nail polish.

Here was the most wonderful creature in the world, and I was hurting her. All these plans we made — and I couldn't follow through on them.

I needed to be alone to figure out a plan. I told her she had to move the car.

"You left it by Emergency. It'll get a ticket."

"Who cares if we get a ticket."

I told her it won't take more than fifteen minutes, that I wasn't going anywhere.

As soon as she left, I called the Boys and told them what I needed. Right now.

If I had nitro, that clock would be dust!

I waited for Bronwyn to get back before I made the next call.

"Hey, Mom. It's Sean. Just wanted to say hello. And, eh, I got a girlfriend."

I held the phone out to Bronwyn. "Wanna say somethin'?"

"Oh! Of course. Hi there . . . Are you there?"

"It's her voicemail."

"Oh. Ha. Well, I look forward to meeting you in person someday."

Bronwyn pressed the phone into the pillow. "You're going to tell her, right?"

I took the phone. "Ya, wait till you meet Bronwyn, Mom. Love you."

I hung up 'cause I was scared I was going to lose it.

Since the night at the dump, Bronwyn tolerated the Boys. But when they showed up in the hospital, that threw her. Then she figured out a way to be cool. Teased them. Rode the roller coaster.

The Boys were already high, but not too out of it to realize something was up. Buddy distracted Bronwyn so Arnie could hide one of the bottles of vodka under my pillow. He left the other one in the brown bag. Buddy uncapped it and had a slug.

When the nurse walked in, Buddy shot off his mouth.

"You think if you wear, like, a flour sack, your ass won't get pinched?"

I told him to shut up.

"Underneath that flour sack, I know, the sweetest meat!"

"Jesus, Buddy! Stop that!" I said.

Bronwyn caught the nurse's eye and shook her head. Sisters in the struggle.

"You can't have alcohol in here," the nurse said.

Buddy just sat there holding the bottle, so she picked up a garbage can and held it out. Instead of dropping the bottle in, he handed it over to Arnie.

Nurse Flour Sack left to call Security. Arnie came over to me. He leaned in, and as he hugged me, he slipped the vodka under my pillow. Now I had both bottles.

He whispered in my ear: "Bronwyn's got her red fingernails sunk into you."

I told him it felt good. "There might even be someone desperate enough to fall for you."

He punched my shoulder.

A beefy guy in a pale blue uniform showed up and stood at the door. Buddy joined Arnie, standing at the foot of my bed. God, these guys. When I took up with Bronwyn, I deserted them, but as soon as I called, they came. No matter what you think, it was them who made something of me.

For once, Buddy didn't have anything to say. He pointed at me. Then he gave a big smile and pointed at the gap where his tooth used to be. He squeezed my foot. Then the security guy grumbled, and they left.

When the nurse came back, I told her Bronwyn was staying the night, keeping an eye on me..So we wouldn't need her. No deal. She said she'd still check in. She showed Bronwyn the call button. Closed the door.

I pulled out the bottle in the brown bag. As soon as she saw it, Bronwyn tried to wrestle it out of my hand. I wouldn't let go.

"No, you can't eat or drink anything before your surgery."

I said, "One shot, that's it."

"You've been doing so well," she said.

She was wavering — I could always see her fault line. I slipped in the charge.

"Don't make me drink alone."

A wet sigh. Boom!

She left to get glasses. While she was gone, I managed to guzzle most of the other bottle. I tried to look innocent when she came back. She poured two modest shots.

"To us," I said.

When it came to drinking hard liquor, Bronwyn was a lightweight. But I coaxed her into having a second and then poured her a third. Finally she got all weepy, popped the hair clip, shook her head. Hair tumbled down like a sandcastle. She made a nest against me and passed out. I looked at Bronwyn. I hadn't been that close to crying since I was a little squirt.

Snore a little louder, pretty one. Drown out the clock. God bless that nurse. A little knock first so I could hide the bottle. She bought it that we were sleeping. She checked me, fiddled with the IV, and left. I had been counting on the double impact of whatever drug they'd given me and the booze to carry me all the way out. When the second bottle was almost empty, I realized I didn't have enough vodka. It was a horrifying realization. Even though Bronwyn was warm beside me, I felt utterly alone. I looked around for something to help me do the job.

My feet hit the cold floor. The IV pulled my arm back. I yanked it out. Pushed off the bed, then the wall. It was a hard slog to the other side of the room. The clock was a long stretch up. My fingertips teased it off the hook. I couldn't believe when I caught it.

I put the clock on the floor, covered it with a pillow. I used one of Bronwyn's cowboy boots to smash the glass cover. Then I put it back beside the other one. Turquoise soldiers standing guard.

The shards hurt going down. They got caught. So I drank more vodka as a chaser. It stung, and I coughed up blood. With the last slug, I washed a long sliver down. It stopped hurting. I lay back down and looked over at Bronwyn. She was a bad splinter. She'd worked her way inside me. Her hair was covering her face, hair I could stroke forever. It was soft like feathers on the underside of a partridge.

This tug of war needs to end. That team is working hard to pull me back. I give a mighty yank. The rope unbraids, and I'm free. The fight is over, and I've won. I sail back and out and up. With Dad.

You'll get past it, Bronwyn, you'll get over me. You deserve a better man.

CABIN BY THE SEA

On the phone, the ticket agent asked Cassie where she was.

"Downtown Halifax."

"What I'd suggest is that you walk down to the harbour and take the ferry across. Our bus picks up at the Dartmouth ferry terminal. It'll cost you three bucks, but you'll save seven on your bus ticket. Plus," she added, "you get a nice ride across the harbour."

Cassie jumped at the idea of a ferry ride. It was a perfect autumn afternoon with a tantalizing coolness in the air, the promise of change.

First she stood on the stern watching the city of Halifax become smaller. The water smelled fresh as it churned over. She'd read online that the municipality had completed its cleanup of the harbour. From now on, they were relying on the harbour to rejuvenate itself. The ocean would perform a tidal cleanse, two times each day.

Cassie had no help with her rejuvenation. Two earthquakes, landing one after the other, had destabilized her — the loss of her father and the breakup with Randall. On top of this, an unanticipated aftershock: her mother, still playing the grieving widow, seemed bent on destroying her. Returning to Nova Scotia, Cassie had counted on her good friends to smooth out her jagged edges. But her besties deprived her of drunken rants and teary revelations by moving away. Cassie desperately needed to flee the city so she booked the weekend off, antagonizing her co-workers at the restaurant. She was running away to be rejuvenated by the ocean.

There were rituals at the family cabin that she could count on to calm her down. Since she was little, she'd sneak off in the morning to study the flat calm of the harbour. Schools of minnows would reveal themselves by churning up the water. Occasionally she'd discover what drove them up to the surface — a seal would bounce up, its whiskered mouth opening and closing. Often she saw the hump of a harbour porpoise rise like a crescent moon. By midmorning, winds made the ocean choppy and the magic was gone.

Meals were cooked on a wood stove, and her chore was to carry in endless armloads of wood. She also hauled water in buckets from the well. When darkness fell, lamps were lit, the Coleman and kerosene. Falling asleep, she listened to the rhythmic clapping of the waves outside. When it was stormy, she could hear the sea suck the stones back and hurl them up again. Their little strip of beach would have to be cleared again.

Cassie left the ferry's stern and made her way, swaying, to the bow. She bent over the rail and looked down. There were sensuous swells of water on both sides of the prow, two perfectly round buns. It reminded her something. What was it? Ah, the painting of a plump bum on the tobacco tin in Uncle Fulton's store. It had the slogan *Nothing Smoother Than a Baby's Bottom.*

By the time the ferry docked in Dartmouth, Cassie felt calm. It was as if some great celestial spatula had descended on her choppy sea and smoothed down all her agitated whitecaps. Sure enough, right outside the ferry terminal, the stop for the Eastern Shore bus was clearly marked.

There were more than a dozen others waiting for the bus, a bubbly group who knew each other. Cassie listened to them chat about their work, families, the mild fall weather. Some of them had city jobs and made this trip daily. Others were heading "up home" for the weekend. Many shifted full shopping bags, having been to town to stock up. Cassie felt twinges of jealousy at their familiarity. Although her father had been raised on the shore, she'd been born and brought up in the city. Unless she married someone from the shore or lived there permanently, she would never be accepted. As she studied them, pretending not to, there was something out of place. What was it? Aha — not one of them was gazing down at a cellphone. And another thing: she wanted them to form a queue like people did in Toronto.

When the old bus pulled up, she discovered that standing in line wasn't necessary. There was an established order that everyone knew, everyone except her. She waited while an elderly woman was helped on first. A bucket line formed to pass up her heavy shopping bags. As each passenger entered, Cassie heard the driver's voice confirming their destinations: Musquodoboit Harbour, Liscomb Mills, Oyster Pond. The names were both familiar and exotic.

Cassie let everyone else enter first. She didn't see the driver until she had mounted the three rickety steps. He wore a lacklustre uniform and a weathered cap, studded with flag pins. He jerked his head quickly to one side, and she recognized it as a greeting, the Eastern Shore nod. Then she realized it wasn't that at all. He was asking, Where are you going?

"Um, the turnoff right after the store?" Cassie heard that she was mumbling. "There's a pull-off and a path to the harbour . . ."

"Which harbour?" the driver asked. "The shore is lousy with harbours."

"Ship Harbour. East Ship Harbour."

"Okay, that's a start." He lowered his head, raised his eyebrows.

She tried again. "That old store? Closed now. Belonged to . . ."

"Fulton Monk. Yep, east side Ship Harbour — where the murderer is. Just got out."

"Murderer?" she asked.

"Old Shamus, Shamus McPhee," the driver said.

The bus shook. Cassie felt the presence of a late passenger crowding in on the steps behind her. The hair on her neck stood up. Behind her, the new passenger panted heavily.

The driver pointed to the front seat where the old woman perched, surrounded by her shopping bags.

"Ya move up here when we're after gettin' to the head a Ship Harbour."

The news that McPhee was a murderer hit her like a sledgehammer. She remembered him well. A dense cluster of spruce trees separated their cabin from McPhee's property. He lived in a saltbox house that was built at a time of few windows, when a view was less important than keeping out the cold. Like a lot of others on the shore, his house was weathered but would never get new paint.

Their father had warned them to steer clear of McPhee. Cassie and her younger brother, Blair, would sneak past the old codger's house, sticking to the shore to get to the clam bed. One year they went picking chanterelle mushrooms. Their father, Bennie Monk, liked them fried up in butter. But as they picked, they wandered near McPhee's house. They heard a loud bang, and something whistled through the trees above their heads.

Their father was caulking the water-logged rowboat. Cassie watched his face harden as they described the incident. As instructed, Cassie and Blair waited inside the cabin with their mother while Bennie went, alone, for a chat with McPhee. Nobody made a peep, listening for the rifle. Finally Bennie opened the door and walked to his favourite armchair. Cassie and Blair pulled over chairs from the kitchen table. Over a cup of strong tea, he measured his words.

"In life, kids, you're not going to get along with everybody. You try to be heard, and you got to listen to them too. But if you can't understand and can't make yourself understood, then you got to clear out of their way."

Lonnie liked this time of day best for walking, after the sun's heat was gone and before the night chill. Nothing felt better than stretching his legs on this old highway, up over the hill from his house, past the graveyard and church and government wharf, then back home again. About an hour round trip. The low sun flashed through the trees, stabbing his eyes. Every day, every single day that he was away, he longed for this, so bad sometimes his legs jerked like he had a hundred amp current running through him.

A lump on the road ahead that shouldn't be there — what it was he couldn't make out. Then as he came up to it, he could see it was a bird and it was dead. His mother's voice rattled at him. "Don't touch, Lonnie. Birds got fleas." Well, his mother wasn't here and he was and then the bird was cradled in the palm of his hand. Perhaps it was a common sparrow, but he couldn't be sure. He didn't know the names of things that lived on land like he knew the name of everything in the sea. This bird was definitely dead. The head rolled to one side, and Lonnie refused to look into the glassy eye. Once, not long ago, the bird could leap off a branch and soar up above the tree, but never again.

Lonnie walked down the slope into the drainage ditch and up the other side to the woods. He found a birch with a low limb and placed the bird softly on the branch. Something would find it and feed on it. On his walk tomorrow, he'd check for feathers and bones.

The bird meant nothing. It was still a sunny evening, no rain, no fog. The dead bird was not a bad sign.

Cassie headed down the aisle toward the rear. What did the driver say? That Shamus McPhee was out of prison and had returned home, to the house that was right beside the cabin, a short walk from where she would be tonight, alone. Near the back of the bus, she found an empty row.

Suddenly it felt as if someone was blowing cold air on her neck. Cassie shivered and glanced behind her. On the back bench seat, two teens were sitting close to one another. The boy, about sixteen, threw his arm over the girl's shoulder. She shoved it off and turned away from him. Cassie quickly faced front. She remembered the out-of-control emotions of first love. First kiss, first rebuke, the terror of being loved, the horror of being rejected. It was all scary and intense — a state of insanity. She was a late bloomer, eighteen, when she fell in love for the first time. It her mother's fault for suggesting she take the real estate course by an expert from "up Toronto." Randall swooped down on her like a seagull, plucked her off the rocks, and flew her up to Toronto with him. She was a mussel that he pecked open, and finally, when he was stuffed, he soared up high and dropped her on the asphalt where she split wide open.

The bus arrived at the first cove, and Cassie saw that the tide was low. At least this was predictable, the big, wide ocean surging in and being sucked out every day. It was always like this and hopefully always would be.

A bed of glistening rockweed lay like a golden garden from the mid-tide mark to where the water receded. She wondered if rockweed was still being harvested. When she was fifteen, she was startled by a dory appearing close to shore. A fisherman with a long-handled rake was standing in the boat. She'd called out to him, asked if he was taking the seaweed to fertilize his garden. He pointed at Cassie and said she was going to eat it. Cassie made a drawn-out groan of disgust, a sound she'd perfected as a teenager.

He asked, "Ya eat jam? Ice cream? This here seaweed is in them things."

Another memory rose up. She had gone out on the Cape Islander with her cousins, Ernie and the other one. What was his name — the one with the limp? Her job was to band the lobsters' claws. A big lobster snapped and sliced her finger. The cut wasn't bad; what hurt was how he laughed at her, the one with the limp. He often visited them at the cabin and stayed longer than anyone else. Her mother had warned her not to stare. He had a withered arm and he spoke with a stutter but, her mother warned, there was nothing wrong with his mind.

Tomorrow at low tide, Cassie promised herself, she'd take a bucket and go down to pull mussels off the rocks. Maybe she'd even put on the mask and snorkel and dive for oysters. Was it too late for the goose tongue? Yes, the shoots would be woody this late in the season.

In tiny communities along the coast, the bus pulled over again and again. Passengers stepped off into twilight, and as the light diminished, they dissolved into darkness. Cassie realized it would be pitch-black when the bus got to Ship Harbour. A dull dread rose up in her as she realized she had not brought a flashlight. She hadn't bothered recharging her cellphone because there was no signal at the cabin. But she'd need the flashlight on the phone. The trail to the cabin twists around boulders and weaves through tall trees. She hoped there would be enough juice left in her phone to light the way.

By the time they arrived at the head of Ship Harbour, Cassie saw that she was the only passenger left — save for the young couple, now interwoven on the back bench, wiggling like an eel.

The church was looming ahead when Lonnie heard the loon call from the harbour. Loons he knew — they were more sea than land. They mated for life. He didn't have a mate, not anymore. Anita hadn't waited, even though at first she'd said she would. Already she was pregnant with Lester's kid. He couldn't blame her; for a while there, it looked bad for him. The loon's call made him feel lonely.

The trouble with being here, being back home, was that nobody knew how to be with him. They were friendly, but after the opening greetings they gave him a wide berth. No one asked where he'd been or what he'd been up to because they already knew. He tried to talk to his mother, but she just said, "There, there," as if he had skinned his knee. He didn't have a skinned knee — he'd done something big and he was all alone with it. In his dreams, there was an older person, a mother or a father, with him and they understood. Sometimes they'd hold him in a tight hug. But when he woke up, he'd get a queer crawling in his stomach. To be alone with himself was terrifying.

Those weeks after the funeral when Cassie lived with her mother, they spoke only when it was essential. It was just the two of them, getting by as best they could. Blair was two hours away at the agricultural college in Truro, but he wouldn't drive down to see his mother and sister. One morning over breakfast, Cassie wondered out loud why he wouldn't visit. Her mother shrugged. Then she asked Cassie why she hadn't phoned during her two years in Toronto, how it would have meant so much to her father.

"He should have phoned me," Cassie said. "I would have accepted his apology."

Her mother shook her head and didn't say anything for a long time. Then, "You're like him, so stubborn."

It was the day Cassie was starting her new job. Determined not to overreact, she left her breakfast plate, untouched, by the sink. Standing in the open door, Cassie stood motionless so she could hear her mother's quiet voice.

"Every night. He sat on the deck, chain-smoking. Wouldn't come up to bed. As if that was good for his health."

Cassie shot back, "So I killed him. Is that what you're saying?"

During lunch break on that first day at the restaurant, she looked for an apartment. Now she had it, a very small and too empty place. She boasted that she didn't need furniture, but the truth was that she couldn't afford much after food, bus fare, and rent.

Her father had said a young adult will leave home quietly or with the slam of a door. When she left with Randall, she slammed the door. Leaving her mother, she tried to close the door quietly, but the rift was there. Why did her parents, the living and the dead, cause her so much grief?

A fog bank oozed in from the harbour and crept across the highway. With it came the sharp tang of salty eel grass and the earthy stench of rotting rockweed. To Cassie, the smell was restorative. In Toronto, whenever she was agitated, she'd eat dulse to calm herself down. Randall would say that her breath stank and make her brush her teeth. Inside the ancient bus, Cassie inhaled the sea air like a healing balm. It made her surrender. She felt submerged in the ocean, wrapped in its familiar chilly warmth.

Cassie hadn't been to the cabin since she'd left for Toronto two years ago. It had been her father's kingdom; he ruled it like an emperor, and the rest of the family fell in line. When Cassie chose Randall, it was as if Bennie declared a holy war against him. Cassie had good reason to slam the door when she left. Still, she felt a stab of regret that there had been no truce. Father and daughter had lost each other in the standoff.

When did the friction between them begin? Cassie recalled the first time she'd crossed her father. In their teen years, she and Blair were hanging out in the cabin's back room. They sat on opposite ends of the bed, her back to the door. She had put on the Eastern Shore accent and was practising expressions.

"You're as stupid as a fart in a mitten."

She'd get Blair to repeat after her with an accent, and they'd both laugh.

"You're as useless as a bag of hammers."

Cassie got up and crossed the room dragging a leg, mimicking the guy with the limp.

"He's that stunned he'd piss the bed awake."

But this time Blair didn't laugh. She turned and there was her father, towering in the doorway. Cassie was scolded for belittling her cousin, and she was put on dish duty for a week.

What condition would the cabin be in, Cassie wondered. Nobody had been there since her father's death in the spring. She and Blair planned on a few days there after their father's funeral. But then Blair bowed out. His excuse was that his baby was teething and his wife needed him. A teething baby, Cassie thought. Give me a break. She asked her mother to come with her and was shocked when her mother said she never liked the cabin. It was Benny's sanctuary, not hers. Without power and running water, making meals and doing laundry were drudgery. She proclaimed that she would never go there again. How was it that all these years Cassie had never guessed that her mother felt this way?

They were getting close now. As soon as Fulton's store was in sight, she'd move up to the front. Fulton Monk was her father's uncle, and in Cassie's eyes, he'd always been ancient. When her father was going to Fulton's store, she and Blair always insisted on going too. To pick out their meat, Uncle Fulton would lead them along the outside of the store, down a steep slope to the rear. They would enter the butchery through a thick door beneath the store. It stayed cool there, even on the hottest summer days. Huge slabs of meat hung from the ceiling. As a child, Cassie thought the sides of beef and pork looked like bad people in hell. Uncle Fulton's huge hands would unhook a slab of bacon. He'd saw it into thick slices that their father said was the best bacon in the world.

Uncle Fulton wasn't shy about telling Bennie what he should and shouldn't do.

"Ya gots to cover that well, Bennie, afore one of them kids falls in and gets drowned."

The last time she heard the warning, Fulton was wrapping bacon in brown paper. He circled the package twice with string. Cassie was waiting for the snap that would come when he made a quick tug to break the string. But the snap didn't happen.

"Did ya build a cover for that well yet, Bennie?"

Her father shifted his pipe to the other side of his mouth. "No, Fulton. But I found a solution. I got the kids wearing life jackets."

Snap.

Through the fog, Cassie saw the outline of the store, the silhouette of the tin Coca-Cola sign. She stood and shouldered her backpack. It was a compact pack but heavy with three days of food and several books. That was pretty much all she brought. She'd be alone so what did it matter if she wore the same clothes every day. Her only regret was that she didn't have room to squeeze in a battery-powered radio. Being alone without music would be tough.

In the mirror, the driver saw her coming and switched on a light above the exit door. When she was within his sight, he twisted in his chair and looked at her. She heard him whistle.

"You're after bein' a Monk! You're Bennie's girl! When did ya get so big?"

Cassie grinned in spite of herself. "Big?"

"Growed up, I mean." He became serious. "Sad t'ing that. I knowed him since he was little. He was a good man, Bennie Monk."

Her father's name, spoken with reverence by a stranger. Four months had passed since he died, yet Cassie felt the shock as if she had just answered the phone and was hearing the news. It warmed her to hear the driver say he was a good man.

"I'm Earl, by the way," the driver said. "I knows your place. About five miles — I mean kilometres."

She swung her pack down onto the nearest seat and sat on the very edge.

"You not a-scared, what with that murderer outta jail. He lives right near your spot. Course you'd know old Shamus McPhee."

"Dad called Mr. McPhee an ornery bastard."

Earl twisted in his seat to look at her. "He done us all a favour when he kilt him, that Lonnie."

"Lonnie?" Cassie jolted back against her pack. "Lonnie killed McPhee?"

Lonnie was the guy she went lobster fishing with, the one who laughed at her. That was his name. Lonnie was her cousin, the one with the expressions she had mimicked.

Earl was eager to tell the story. "How come you never heared? Happened two years ago."

Cassie nodded — the biggest event on the Eastern Shore happened when she was in Toronto. She leaned forward so she wouldn't miss a word.

"So McPhee, he got himself a brand-new red Ford pickup. He didn't have no need for it, except to show off. He just drove that rig up an' down the highway. God help anyone who got in his way. And that Lonnie Monk, always walking the road. McPhee woulda claimed Lonnie got in his way. According to Lonnie, he was just walking the shoulder like always when McPhee come up from behind. He pulled over far enough that his big side mirror banged Lonnie in the ditch. Soon as his shoulder was better, Lonnie paid McPhee a visit. McPhee come to the door wit' his rifle. There was a scuffle. Lonnie got the rifle — and shot McPhee."

"That's how McPhee died?"

"Not yet. He didn't kill him. McPhee got the door bolted. He was too tight to own a phone, so he was on his own. Lonnie waited with the rifle outside the door late into the night, listening to the old man thrash around inside. When he didn't hear no more noise, he busted down the door. McPhee was dead on the floor. Now, how he got caught . . ."

Earl shot another look at Cassie and saw her eager nod.

"Lonnie stole them keys to the truck, headed to the border. He never been off Nova Scotia, see? He drove right slow, so he wouldn't get caught speedin'. Past Amherst to the Isthmus o' Chignecto. That's where the Mounties spotted him, on the Tantramar Marshes. Why would someone drive a brand-new truck that slow? When they pulled him over, Lonnie said, 'I done it. I killed him.'"

She heard the blinker signal. The bus slowed.

"The cops didn't know what he was on about. Nobody knew McPhee was dead. They had a Mountie drive over here from Sheet Harbour. There was McPhee, dead on his kitchen floor."

Earl eased onto the shoulder and stopped. "And that's the truth of it."

Cassie's heart was beating so hard she worried that Earl might see it. She heard her voice, too loud. "Why would they let him out?"

"Calm down!" Earl said in a long, drawn-out way: *cal-mmm*. "It weren't premeditated. Self-defence is what he done. And your father was right about McPhee. Old bastard weren't nothin' but grief. We're better off wit'out em."

Earl pulled the lever, and the door swung open. Cassie's pack seemed heavier now. In the light that spilled out, she saw the first few feet of the trail. Beyond that, darkness.

"You takin' the bus back Monday morning?"

"Yes. Are you the driver?"

He shrugged. "I don't see nobody else stupid enough ta do it. At least I keeps my grandson here outta trouble. That's him on the back bench pawing his girl. They gets off just up the road."

Cassie wondered if everyone on the shore was connected in some way. She started down the steps.

"So I gets here at 7:50," Earl said. "If you're not here waitin', I'll figure . . ."

He waited until she turned around to face him.

"I'll figure Lonnie got ya."

Earl's raucous laughter followed Cassie off the bus. Outside, she turned to say something, but the door was already stuttering shut. The peeling green paint slid past her. She watched the bus lumber down the narrow highway until it was gone, and all that was left was the briny air and the blackness.

Lonnie heard the bus coming long before it arrived. When it pulled over, he wasn't surprised to see Alex get off. Some girl waved goodbye through the door until Earl barked at her to "Leave off now." She pulled back inside and Ernie peeled out, if an old bus can peel.

Already Lonnie had heard updates on Alex, his young cousin, that he was sweet on a girl from up the shore, a distant relative. The flames burning so high everyone was scared he'd soon have her in the family way. Leave it to Earl to sidetrack his grandson by taking him and the girlfriend for rides on the bus. How much trouble could they get into on a public bus?

"Hi there, little cuz," Lonnie called out, limping over to Alex as fast as he could. The boy turned and said hey and then just stared at him. Lonnie squirmed as the silence settled around them like the cold night. Young people have a low tolerance for discomfort, and Lonnie knew he had only seconds to connect to the boy or he'd lose him.

"What's new in the big city?"

Predictably Alex shrugged. "Nothin'."'

"Anyone interestin' on the bus?"

"Nope." Alex turned toward the gravel driveway leading to his trailer. But instead of walking away, he turned around.

"A girl got off at the Monk cabin, Benny Monk's. Grandad says she's too green to last long. Too citified."

As Alex went down the driveway, he triggered a bright light on the trailer. The intensity of the beam made Lonnie feel guilty. He wanted to be home now.

Cassie turned and stared toward where she guessed the trail started. What she needed was a full moon, high enough to cast light, but the sky was crowded with dense fog. When she switched on her cellphone, the battery bar was a tiny red line and there was no signal. Following the phone's flashlight beam, she started down the path, weaving around the trees. A night hawk squawked and startled her.

The beam did not dim; it went from bright to suddenly off. She stopped to wait for her eyes to adjust. The fog made the trees look like dark witches in black robes, reaching out to her with scratchy arms. Slowly she fumbled forward. Before she expected it, the cabin loomed ahead of her, a bleak form against a dark sky. It stopped her in her tracks. This was how it looked in her dream, the dream she'd had in Toronto. In the dream, it was a dark night like this. She had the sensation that something was missing: where was her father? She didn't know how she could be there without him — it made no sense. He was always there. There was danger in the wind. Seagulls wheeled and screamed in the blustery sky. The gusts bent the wild irises flat, and the sea was spitting froth onto the shore. She knew a hurricane was coming. She ran around shuttering the windows. When she turned and faced the horrific wind, she knew she couldn't save herself from whatever was coming. She woke terrified, panting.

Randall had been no comfort and told her to go back to sleep. She was still awake at dawn when the phone rang; her father had had a stroke and wasn't expected to recover.

Cassie pleaded with Randall to come with her to the funeral. He said it would be best if he wasn't there to lean on. That way, she'd sink completely into the grief so that when she returned she would be over it. He wouldn't want her sulking around, feeling sorry for herself.

After some weeks in Nova Scotia, Cassie kept returning to Randall instructing her on how to grieve. She remembered looking up at him, teary-eyed, and nodding. In that moment, she'd thought Randall was wise. She saw the world through his eyes and could almost predict what he'd say and do. When she decided not to return to him, her only regret was that she wouldn't be with Randall when he lost a parent. She wanted to instruct him to process quickly: no sulking, get over it.

Getting into the cabin was a series of hurdles. The screen door was stuck; she yanked on it until it finally swung open. The padlock's shank was rusted; she banged it with a rock until the shank broke. When she pushed the door open, it stuck on a warped floorboard. She had to remove her pack and angle in sideways. It was cold inside, and she looked forward to having a fire in the cookstove.

She found the flashlight by feel, on the hook by the door. The beam was weak and fluttered like a butterfly. Tomorrow she'd try her father's trick, sticking a wad of tinfoil at the end of the batteries. The candles on their saucers weren't in the cupboard where they were usually stored. She fumbled in a drawer for candles, and memories of her childhood bumped her fingers: tangled twines of kite string, brown paper bags with fishhooks protruding, boxes of crayons, matches but no candles. There was nothing on the mantle above the fireplace but an old, quiet alarm clock. Cassie wondered if it had batteries that she could use in the flashlight but realized it didn't run on batteries; it was a wind-up clock. On the counter, she found what was left of the candles. Some critters had been busy: the wax was chewed off and lay in crumbly bits at the base of stiff, useless strings. Strange that the candles hadn't been put away. Before leaving, Bennie had his closing-up rituals. Her favourite was that he'd sprinkle coffee grounds on the floor to keep the dust down. She never saw him sweep a floor except at the cabin.

Well, the rodents couldn't get at the Coleman lamp. The thought of lighting the lamp intimidated her, but she'd watched her father do it since she was little. The darkness outside the small circle of the flashlight's beam scared her more. Her mind flashed on Lonnie, and fear licked at her innards. She was a sitting duck here, waiting to be murdered. No, she argued with herself, calm down. Her inner voice said it the way Earl had: Cal-mmm down, Cassie.

When she lifted the lamp from its hook, she knew from its weight that the tank was empty. Ever since she was a kid, her father would instruct them: "Leave the cabin ready for your return." Why hadn't he filled the lamp before he left? Had his health been failing before the stroke? He was fifty-three, too young to be forgetting things. She carried the Coleman, the tank of camp fuel, and a funnel out to the deck. It was another of his edicts — always light the lamp outside.

Far away in the dark harbour, a loon called. She knew about loons, that they had four calls. This was the wail, and it always sounded like desperate yearning. Now it made her feel intensely lonely. She'd never been at the cabin without her entire family. In her whole life, when had she ever been alone? She'd gone from the family home to living with Randall, then returned to the family home until her mother started picking on her. The new apartment was scuzzy from all the people who had lived there before her. It made her feel alien, like a visitor on the planet. The feeling had followed her to the cabin. Hell, twenty years old and she was only now learning how to be alone. How weird was that?

A chill wind in furtive gusts was coming off the water. Cassie remembered that there was a pattern: after sunset, the wind shifted so it no longer blew offshore. Now it came onshore, gathering cool air from the harbour. Cassie felt reassured that she hadn't forgotten this, the rhythms of land and sea and wind. It gave her confidence that she was meant to be here. She placed the old lamp on the deck. By feel, she found and unscrewed the fuel cap and stuck the plastic funnel into the tank. The fuel was gurgling into the chamber when a gust of wind lifted the funnel and blew it away. Cassie felt the cold kerosene soak into her jeans. She heard the funnel bounce off the deck into the dark. She found the cap and screwed it back on. In the morning, she'd find the funnel. In the morning, she'd heat water to wash her only pair of jeans. Hopefully enough fuel made it into the tank to get her through the night. Her father always pumped one hundred strokes of air into the chamber; she was pleased when she managed ninety-two. She screwed the valve tight.

It was definitely too windy to light the lamp on the deck, so she carried it inside. Where was the safest place to light the lamp? The aluminum sink. When she turned the lever to the Light setting, the familiar hiss of gas. She brought the lit match toward the lamp. Suddenly, flames were shooting up to the ceiling. The fuel on the outside of the tank had ignited. Even the wire handle, standing up, was engulfed.

Cassie's first thought was that the fuel tank might explode. She had to get the lamp outside. She pulled on an oven mitt and reached into the flames, grabbing the handle. Holding the lamp out in front of her, she hurried to the door. She yanked hard to pull the door over the warped floorboard. When she set the lamp on the deck rail, flames jumped to her soiled jeans. For a panicked moment, she saw herself, her whole body, a towering pillar of fire, weaving across the rocks toward the harbour, stumbling and falling just short of the water. This was how she would die.

No! Cassie rejected the image. With the oven mitt, she patted the flames until she got them out. Worried that the lamp might set the deck on fire, she grabbed the handle and pitched the lamp. It was a strange sight, the orange object careening through the air, somersaulting end over end. The flames on the forward side waned, the fire on the back glowed. The glass mantle shattered when the lamp landed on the boulders. She could see by the light of the dying flames that it was above the high tide mark. In the morning, she would retrieve it. Where could she find a replacement mantle for the 1950s lamp? She watched, panting, as the fuel burned off and the flames died, leaving her in darkness.

Cassie removed her jeans while she was still outside. One of her thighs was stinging. Her fingers fumbled along the hot skin. In the darkness, she couldn't tell how badly she was burned. She rolled up her sooty, smelly jeans and left them there on the deck. What would she wear when she left? she wondered.

The cabin refused to give her any comfort. The chill wind that blew off the harbour shoved dampness through the cracks. She shone the flashlight on the stack of wood piled near the stove. To start a fire, she'd need kindling. There wouldn't be enough light outside, so that would mean chopping it here, on the kitchen floor. She was never good at chopping wood; she envisioned her hand holding a chunk on the block and the axe sinking into her hand. Did she want to risk another injury? No.

In her meagre supplies, the only food that didn't need cooking was the can of beans, but cold beans were totally unappealing. The heat on her thigh was intense now. What she should do is put something cold on it. Even a damp cloth would help. The water bucket was upside down beside the sink, but the well was a scary walk away, around at the back of the cabin. What if the flashlight died while she was out there by the well? What if she fell in? Without a life jacket, she'd drown just like Uncle Fulton said. She heard herself chuckle. The sound was loud and scary, like a clown in a horror movie.

It was still early, not even nine yet. What would she do for the rest of the evening? She could think of nothing else but to go to bed. Pulling back the comforter, she found a peppering of black specks on the bedsheet. Mice droppings — she hoped they hadn't made a nest in the bed. She'd sleep on top of the quilt in a sleeping bag.

Despite her fleece jacket, she lay there shivering. The sleeping bag was damp and icy cold. The only heat was on her thigh, and her fingers found blisters beginning to rise.

Self-loathing invaded her. She had been tested and had not passed. Her screw-ups demonstrated that she could not manage here on her own. There was no option, she decided, but to return to the city in the morning. With no bus until Monday, she'd have to hitchhike. Yes, it was dangerous, but less scary than staying. If her incompetence didn't destroy her, Lonnie would come by with a shotgun and finish her off. Where did Lonnie live? She used to know. A house just over the hill?

Where was the axe? She remembered seeing it leaning against the wall beside the stove. She fetched it and propped it up by the bed, leaning against the dresser. It was within arm's reach — if Lonnie broke in to murder her, she could try to defend herself.

As Cassie's body heat warmed the sleeping bag, the shivering stopped. She found that if she stretched out an arm or leg, she'd be assaulted by the cold again so she had to lie still. She grew used to the silence.

In her dream, she heard the wail of a loon. It was the call a loon uses to locate members of its family. Fog on the harbour prevented her from seeing the loon, but she knew it was her father. She wanted to get closer, but a cold choppy sea kept them apart. She wanted to yell at him to stop being so standoffish, to come closer. She tried to say that she heard and that she was near, but the words were like dry sand in her mouth.

A noise woke her. The soft light of pre-dawn barely illuminated the cabin. What was that sound? A regular rhythm — a ticking. When Cassie realized that it was the clock, she sat bolt upright. The only person who could have wound the clock was her, and she hadn't touched it. Cassie leaped from the bed. She strode to the mantle, and her fingers grasped the clock. She held it in both hands and read the time: 6:33. She shook it, but it wouldn't stop. The ticking filled the whole cabin. She found something to bang it against — her father's armchair. She whammed it down, again and again.

When she stopped, the clock no longer made a peep. The cover was shattered, and splinters of glass were imbedded in her father's sacred chair. She watched the shards fall and land on the floor. She became aware that her hands stung and her arms ached, but she was fixated on the time on the clock. What was it about that number? 6:33. Then she remembered why it was familiar. When she'd seen the death certificate, everything had been incomprehensible but the date — April 6 — and the time — 6:33 — as if these numbers were concrete enough to resurrect her father.

Cassie returned to bed. As she curled up tight, she could make out the dresser standing like a soldier beside the bed. She remembered some clothes were kept there, a haphazard assortment of shirts and pants. Maybe there was some musty pair of pants she could wear.

Rapping on the door woke her. Cassie's first thought was that it was her father and she wondered that he was outside. Wasn't he inside the cabin with her?

"You in there?"

It was a voice she recognized from her childhood — Lonnie. What could she do? If there was a deadbolt, she could shove it over. She wiggled out of the sleeping bag and raced to the door.

"I heared you come back," he said.

There was no bolt. The only barrier between her and the murderer was a flimsy wooden door.

"That was my nephew, on the bus with yous. He said Earl dropped a girl off here and I figured it out. Cassie, right?"

She envisioned the axe beside the bed in the room behind her.

"Just a minute!"

She stopped, frozen, her arms by her sides staring at the axe leaning against the dresser. She realized she was wearing only her jacket and panties.

The voice from outside. "A nice cup of tea would be in order. Always a comfort, right?"

He wasn't going away. In the dresser she found a pair of her father's work pants and pulled them on.

When Cassie opened the door, she watched Lonnie limp in and close the door behind him. He looked around, sniffing the air.

"Some cold in here. Your fire died?" he said.

She gestured, with open hands, toward the wood stove. "I didn't think I'd bother."

Lonnie crossed to the wood box and thumped around inside it. "Gonna need kindling. Where's the axe to?"

Cassie wheeled around and headed for the bedroom. Lonnie's voice followed her.

"What's the axe doin' way back there? Bennie mighta growed up here, but once he moved down to the city, he got some queer ideas."

They sat across from each other at the kitchen table, the room illuminated with early morning light filtered through fog. Lonnie had made the fire, and Cassie had hauled water from the well. The heat from the wood stove drove the chill away and made Cassie's cheeks flushed. Lonnie had his big cup of steaming tea, and she had her coffee. She'd brought precious little food with her and didn't offer to share for fear of running short.

He asked if he could smoke inside, and she gave him a bowl for an ashtray. Why a bowl? Her father was a smoker, but he used a clamshell. When Lonnie crushed his butt in the bowl, she saw it was her favourite with the happy circles in different colours. He'd desecrated a family heirloom.

"How's your mum doin'?" he asked.

"Good, I guess. Good as can be expected."

"People are always after sayin' dat. 'Good as can be expected.' Your mum worried after Bennie somethin' fierce. Wanted me ta take him fishin'. I asked but he never come out wit' us."

Cassie wondered if he remembered the time she went lobster fishing with him, the time he laughed at her. It was years ago, but she couldn't forgive him. She said nothing.

Lonnie obviously didn't like gaps in conversation.

"I finally got it outta him, why he wouldn't come on the boat. He was waitin' for a call, see, and didn't want his phone to get wet. All these years I seen Bennie here, his work weren't nothin' to him. Then he's scared to miss a call?"

Cassie wanted Lonnie to drink his tea down and leave. She resented that he had sympathy right off for her mother and now he seemed to be siding with her father.

"He weren't da same, after yous left, you and Blair right after. He just sat there."

They both looked around at the chair, Bennie's chair by the fireplace. Cassie hoped the damage she'd done to it couldn't be seen and that Lonnie wouldn't notice the remnants of the clock on the floor. She glanced toward the door and remembered her father standing there. Cassie would be playing outside with Blair, and she'd complain when it wasn't sunny. Bennie had a magic thermostat beside the door frame that only he could see. After he'd turn it up, sure enough the sun would burn through the fog. For a moment she was a child again, looking up at the mountain of a man who was her daddy and loving him with all her little being.

Bennie had told her not to go away with Randall. Cassie heard it as disapproval of her choice. She prodded him until he admitted he didn't like her boyfriend. There were horrid words flung at each other like manure against a wall.

"I'm sorry for your loss, Cassie. Everyone 'round here could see how close you guys was. He was a good man."

"Dad had his faults. He wasn't perfect," she told Lonnie.

"Course he weren't perfect. Nobody's perfect. I met mean people in jail, real mean. Your daddy was a far cry from dem. Me, too, I tells ya, I ain't one a dem."

There was no buildup to it, but suddenly Cassie felt like she'd lost her anchor. She was a rowboat, yanked loose and adrift on the turbulent sea. One moment she was staring at Lonnie, resenting him, and the next she was miserably sad. She gripped the table and got to her feet, hoping Lonnie would get the message and leave. He looked up at her.

"But nobody's all bad. Even old Murphy weren't all bad. He didn't deserve to die. I didn't mean to kill him."

Cassie took a deep breath to stabilize herself. Murphy was the last person she cared about. Her inhalations came in and went out in jagged chunks. At last Lonnie drained his cup and stood up.

"You got your dead, and I got mine."

When he'd left her alone, Cassie was overcome with sadness for her father, her mother, her brother, and herself. They had been a unit, a cohesive whole, like a starfish with independent arms. When she'd slammed the door, she had cleaved them all apart.

As the sun burned through the fog, Cassie's plan to leave dissolved. She had to stay and make this place her own. She'd bring in wood to keep the stove going. She'd chop kindling for when the fire needed to be relit. Those crayons in the drawer could be melted and made into candles. Hadn't she done that when she was a kid? But she was farther from being a kid now than she'd ever been. She felt older, less a child with all the answers and more an adult with questions. Older and more confused.

ACKNOWLEDGEMENTS

Thanks to all my magnificent neighbours on Scotch Corner in Dawson City for honouring the notice I put on the front door: "Caution — rabid writer inside. Particularly infectious between 9am and 2pm":

Linda Glass
Kath Selkirk
Jim Taggert
Debbie Wight

Thanks to local writers and readers who reviewed early drafts and gave great notes:

Saskia Blagaj-Berger
Tara Borin
Danny Dowhal
Louise Dumayne
Karen MacKay
Gaby Sgaga
Chuck Stad

Joann Vriend
Meg Walker
Helen Winton

Thanks for feedback from other writers, friends, and family:

Charlotte Gray
Lawrence Hill
Darren Hynes
Calhoun Keating Malay
Grace Keating
Bernadette Lancaster
Michelle Latimer
Rod Malay
David Wiseman

Huge thanks to Lawrence Hill for generously introducing me to Samantha Haywood at Transatlantic Agency. Thanks, Sam, for graciously taking me on. To Susan Renouf, an enormously gifted editor at ECW Press, who gave me insightful notes with precision and clarity.

Thanks to those who helped with my funding applications: Yasmine Renault and Maria Sol Suarez Martinez. With a grant from the Yukon Government's Culture Quest, I was able to hire Greg Bechtel for preliminary editing of many of the stories, thereby paying him for his feedback instead of buying him drinks at Bombay Peggy's

Thanks to Wade Hemsworth for permission to use lyrics from "The Log Driver's Waltz."

Funding for this project is made possible through the assistance of Culture Quest, Government of Yukon.